Overbooked in Arizona

Overbooked
in
Arizona

A Novella

By Samuel Hirsh Gottlieb

Cover art and illustrations by Joe Servello

Published by
Camelback Gallery
P.O. Box 13476
Scottsdale, Arizona 85267

1994

Library of Congress Cataloging-In-Publication Data

Gottlieb, Samuel Hirsh, 1939-
Overbooked In Arizona / by Samuel Hirsh Gottlieb.
p. cm.
$25
1. Rare books-Collectors and collecting - Arizona - Fiction
2. Murder - Arizona - Fiction. 1. Title
PS3557.0832094 1993   93-33521
813'.54-dc20   CIP

ISBN 0-9639966-1-4 (hrd.cvr.)

Published by Camelback Gallery

Manufactured in the United States of America

This First Hardcover Edition of
Overbooked in Arizona
has been limited to 1501 copies.

To Thomas Berger

Overbooked
in
Arizona

Contents

Part 1
OUT OF CONTROL

F our hours ago, at 5:30 P.M., my team of defense attorneys said good-bye and left my cell for the last time. They had come to tell me that the Ninth Circuit Court of Appeals had turned down my request for a stay of execution, and that the governor's office had refused to consider a last minute plea for clemency. What a shock. A guy had a better chance of being hit by a falling whale in Nebraska than of getting clemency in the State of Arizona.

All of which meant that in a scant two hours and thirty-five minutes the citizens of the great State of Arizona would exact their pound of flesh from me by snuffing out my miserable existence with the injection of a Cactus Country Cocktail. One part sodium pentathol, one part Pavlouvan, one part potassium chloride. Period. No gin, no olive.

Was this possible? Could this really be happening to me? Was I to go down in the history books as the first former Hebrew school teacher ever to have been executed by the State of Arizona? Why? How? I had been consumed with these questions for the past two years now, and I still didn't have an answer.

I can't blame my attorneys. A couple of nice kids, they worked like dogs. In a little bit over their heads; they were overmatched. Bottom line? Simple. They hadn't been able to get a jury to understand the difference between a robbery for money and *my* crime which was the product of my passion for fine books and good literature. Ah well, it was an Arizona jury. What a place. In this state, a book is something that you read to learn how to shoot a gun. My guess is that if you polled every redneck goober who lives here, you couldn't come up with twenty who could tell you who wrote *Moby Dick*. In Arizona, if it doesn't drive, shoot or screw, it's not worth spit.

The governor here is a character known as J. Fife Symington The Third. With a Roman numeral III. The Fifester. A real hootchie cootchie man. He was a big time financier and real estate developer before being elected governor, and one of his last great projects, before he slithered into public office, was to con a bunch of wealthy Hispanic businessmen into investing in some fatally flawed and grossly fraudulent downtown Phoenix shopping mall. This place, known as The Mercado, was to be a shrine to Latino culture, and a huge boon to the seedy downtown area which needed all the boons it could get. Anyway, after a couple of years of flopping and floundering, the place finally went belly-up by filing for "protection from creditors" under every chapter of the bankruptcy code known to man and beast. So, the Fifester, who is still personally on the hook for some of the liability, but who is by now The Governor, tries to pressure the City of Phoenix to put up about five million of its citizen's hard earned potatoes to bail him out. All of this only a few months after he had publicly called for private donations to a legal defense fund to help him out with some other minor problema he was having with the Federales about several billion dollars of taxpayer money which was missing from a savings and loan which he had been directing. He didn't see anything wrong with the notion that these private donations would all come from the folks who were already dining

─────── 6 ───────

at the public trough, or waiting in line to do so. A genuine troglodyte.

But the real hallmark of The Fifester's administration, his glorious two years as Governor of Arizona, was his flat refusal to go along with a federal judge's ruling which had legalized gambling on Indian reservations. He really went to the mat on that issue because, he said, "Gambling is terribly immoral." Except for the thriving horse and dog tracks operating around the state. Not to mention the state lottery. I guess the most immoral part was that the state wasn't going to get its normal twenty percent vigorish from the reservations.

This political stuff is generally pretty boring, and not what anybody in his right mind wants to know about, but I thought you should have the whole background. I told you that earlier today my attorneys had submitted an eleventh hour petition for clemency to this goniff. Well, you can only imagine my delight to have learned that a half hour before receiving my plea, The Fifester got word that the Cocopah Indian tribe from down around Yuma and the tribe from Fort McDowell had made a serious offer to the bankruptcy court to buy his Mercado. Their plan was to turn it into the world's largest gambling casino. Gee, he must have been in a really swell mood when he finally looked over our petition. So, this was the guy who wouldn't grant me clemency. The governor before him was ol' Ev Meacham. A dyed-in-the-wool meshuginah from way back. He was so nuts that even these yahoos were too embarrassed to let him stay in office, and they impeached him. I doubt that he would have granted me any clemency either.

But the real Prince Charming here is the state's attorney general. His name is, are you ready? Grant Woods. I'm serious. No joke. Grant Fucking Woods. Almost exactly like the guy who painted that famous picture called *American Gothic*. Now, Grant Wood might have been an OK name for some weirdo artist from the 1920s who liked to draw silos and haystacks which looked exactly like penises and testicles, but nowadays only a real putz-with-earlaps could walk around with a name like this. But anyway, *this* Grant Woods loves to execute people. In fact, it is thought by many who know him that he would rather be involved in an execution than just about anything else—including sex. Just a few short years ago, he spent two whole days and nights personally driving, flying and running around the state schlepping papers from one judge to another just to make sure some poor jerk named Harding got gassed on schedule. It turned out to have been a horrible and barbaric event, and several of the morning blabs actually began to call for an end to the death penalty. Woods panicked and immediately began to support a bill to have the method of execution switched from the gas chamber to lethal injection. His feverish nonstop TV appearances touting the benefits of injections over gas earned him the nickname "Needles."

"More humane," he said. Mind you, Needles couldn't have cared less about humane. In fact, a large number of people who were close to him let it out that he really much preferred the old cyanide method. It took longer and hurt a lot more, but he was shrewd enough to recognize that if the gas were replaced by injection, there would be fewer protests, and he could get many more executions done in a lot shorter time. This had been proven in Texas where they were now popping them off three at a time. Sort of one great state learning from another.

Just a few months ago, some sixty-five-year-old s.o.b. was convicted of dynamiting a reporter for one of the local blabs about eighteen years earlier. Naturally the press gave the event much coverage, since it seems they get pretty worked up when one of their own guys gets it. Would Needles seek the death penalty? I mean, after all, even a maniac like Woods knew that the appeals process still could go for up to ten years, and who wanted to see some seventy-five-year-old geezer shuffling along with a walker on his last mile? Woods told the breathless press that "Age *is* an issue, and I'll have to think about it." One hour later, the thinking part was over. "Woods To Seek Death In Bowles Case" was all over the front pages. Another big surprise.

Yeah, this Grant Woods is a real sweetheart. He attends all of the dances in person and I know that tonight when they pull the plug on me, he'll be right there. On the fifty yard line. He pulled out all the stops on my case. A genuine cause célèbre. When I first heard that he was personally going to represent the prosecution at my trial, I knew that I had plenty of serious trouble.

But, back to **how**? **Why**? How had my passion for fine books gotten so out of control that I was ending it all in an Arizona penitentiary in a cow town like Florence, Arizona. Surrounded by millions of acres of badlands covered with tumbleweed, scorpions, coyotes and rattlesnakes. Why had the jury not been able to understand that what had happened to me could have happened to any one of them; had they only ever learned how to read.

Let me go back to the beginning. About six years ago. When I first began to appreciate the beauty and value of fine first editions of modern literature. I had just moved to Arizona to "semi-retire" from the San Francisco Bay Area where I had owned a moderately successful soup and sandwich joint which I had sold to Mahmoud and Farhoud Buickzadah, a couple of very crazy Iranian brothers who were both graduates of the culinary school at the

University of Egypt, known affectionately by its alumni as "Farouk U." My idea was that with the low cost of living in Arizona and with all that cash I really wouldn't have to do much of anything. Boy, can that grow old in a big hurry.

But before I go into the specifics of what I refer to as "the incident," and what Needles liked to call "the savage act of a mad-dog killer," it's important that you gain some insight into my fascination with books, and something about books themselves. I don't actually recall exactly how I became so totally immersed in the world of modern literature, but I believe that it all began shortly after my move here to Arizona. I had wandered into an antique shop in Mesa in search of a couple of old chairs which might work in my living room, and on my way out I noticed a bunch of books reposing in a glass case near the cash register. Prominent among these was a copy of *Catcher in the Rye* by J.D. Salinger. I was shocked and amazed to see a price of $1500 on this item. I had, of course, as had all undergraduates of my era, read that book while I was enrolled at The University of Buffalo, and since I never throw anything away, I was certain that I still had it packed away. I raced home and started to rummage through the thirty or so boxes of books I had accumulated over the years. And there it was.

Rocketing back to the antique store with heady anticipation, I gleefully shoved my *Catcher* under the proprietor's nose. An extra $1000 or so would have come in mighty handy at that time, since I had just blown a like amount on the muskrats and polecats which they disguise as racehorses at Turf Paradise Racetrack out on Bell Road here in Phoenix.

The antique guy smiled wanly at me as he looked my book over. I noticed with some chagrin that he handled it as though it were a fresh turd. "Wal," he drawled, "I could pay you 'bout fifty cen' for it. That is," and he showed me a quick mirthless grin, "if I needed it. Which I don't." He then began to explain to me that "First of all, you'rn don't have a dust jacket." This seemed to be a major magillah for him, and he went on to tell me that the dust jacket was worth more than the actual book itself. Next he stated that my book, unlike his, was not a first edition, and in fact was about the worst thing that a book could be. He almost shuddered as he said it: "A book club edition." He pointed to a small square dot neatly pressed into the cloth binding on the back cover at the bottom, and near the spine. "This 'ere mark is called a blind stamp. It's a sure fire sign that you got a Book of the Month Club edition."

"They ain't nothin' worse than a book club edition. All them damn fools out there that belongs to the Book of the Month Club," his wizened face seemed to be contorted with pain, "they all thinks they's gittin' a bargain. Fact is, they's gettin' plumb screwed. The fun part is when they gets tahred of all them books, and they goes to sell 'em. Nobody will take 'em. Not even most charities,—even for free."

A benign smile played around his lips, and he seemed to relax. He gazed heavenward and appeared to go into a sort of trance. He was thinking of those millions of subscribers to the BOMC who were going to find out that their priceless hoard of books, which they had bought for such a great price, were actually worth zip.

I became mesmerized by the intricacies and details, and talked with the old buzzard for almost an hour before he began to tire of giving me a free education. He let me know that his primary interest was in nineteenth century furniture, and that he really didn't do that much with books. He handed me a small brochure, which was entitled *Bookstores of the Greater Phoenix Area,* from a stack on a shelf behind the register. The brochure contained a map of Phoenix and surrounding territories, and a list of all book-stores in that area. The map displayed the location of each shop with a number on the map which corresponded to the numbers on the listing. He circled a few which he said might be good prospects for finding modern first editions, and he told me I should probably go over to Tempe and try a small, relatively new book store there, not too far from Arizona State University. "Lenny's a good guy," he said. "Little pricey, but loves first editions, and knows somethin' 'bout 'em too." This guy spoke like a character from *Tobacco Road*, but he had been helpful, so I thanked him and walked out of his dingy shop into the searing blaze of a Phoenix afternoon in July.

My eyesight began to return after only a few minutes and I found my car right where I had left it. New to the area, I had made the rookie error of leaving my keys in the car. It wasn't an unusually hot day, with the temperature hover-ing right around the 110° mark, but the interior of my trusty silver 1976 Lincoln was really sizzling. As my fingers grasped the key in the ignition, I heard a scream. Shortly, I recognized the voice to be my own, and I sat in amazement watching welts and blisters sprout on my fingers. By that time, I had almost recovered enough of my eyesight to drive, and after finally getting the car started, I headed west on University Avenue toward Tempe.

With the help of the handy map in the brochure, I found College Used Books in about twenty minutes. Without the map, I could have been there in ten. But the antique shop guy had been right. There was a veritable gold mine here of modern literature and fiction, and one full section devoted strictly to first editions. The owner, Lenny Warman, seemed friendly enough, and when I explained to him that I had recently decided to become a collector of rare books but that I was a novice with no real idea of what I was doing, his eyes lit up, and I thought I saw a small stream of saliva dripping from the corner of his mouth. He quickly composed himself, and asked which authors were of particular interest to me, and how much actual cash I had in my pockets.

In the end, Lenny turned out to be a pretty decent guy. Of all the book people I thought I had befriended, he was the only one who testified on my behalf at the trial. His testimony that he might have done just what I did caused a real stir in the courtroom, and he was booed and hissed by everyone including the judge and the jury. He was later forced to resign from the Phoenix Booksellers Association for conduct unbecoming a member, and for his "association with distinctly undesirable types." Warman introduced me to a number of informative publications and journals such as *Firsts Magazine* which were helpful in getting me started, and spent hours teaching me how to judge the condition of a book. "Grading," was what he called it. These lessons included his constant harping about how remainder marks and "price clipped" dust jackets impair the condition and diminish the value of otherwise nice copies of collectible books.

Remainder marks are often applied by a publisher to books which have not sold to retail stores at the regular price, and which the publisher now wants to eliminate from his inventory. They are sold for literally pennies on the dollar to discounters and to bookstores to be sold on "remainder tables" at very low prices. These publishers and retailers want to be able to identify these books so that they cannot be later returned for credit at the original price, and so the books are marked with any number of devices including a simple marking pen, rubber stamp, spray paint, etc. The marks are generally applied to the bottom of the pages, but can be on the top, the sides or even inside the books.

Some pretty valuable books are around with remainder marks from the days before the author became salable. Lenny showed me a copy of Jim Harrison's scarce novel, *A Good Day to Die*, which in spite of the thin remainder line across the bottom of the pages was priced at a snappy $300. He told me that sans the mark, the book could go for as much as $400. He further illustrated his point by pointing to an array of books by Richard Brautigan; all were remainder marked, and priced at about sixty percent of the retail price of similar copies without the mark. It was kind of weird picturing ten or fifteen copies of *A Confederate General From Big Sur* sitting around on a remainder table somewhere for 99¢ apiece, when people are now knocking each other over the head to find them for $150. Sadder still for Brautigan, who had committed suicide at least in part because of his poor sales.

The issue of price clipped dust jackets was also a very hot topic with Lenny. This is something that almost anyone living outside of the State of Arizona, thereby having actually seen a book, has encountered at one time or another. It is a book which has had the price snipped off of the dust jacket. These prices are almost always located on the upper right hand corner of the front end flap of the dust jacket, and the entire corner has been diagonally cut off. This is usually the work of some well-meaning but chintzy relative or friend who gave the book as a gift, but didn't want the recipient to know how little they had spent. What a bunch of cheapos. Did they think that their nieces and nephews were such idiots that they would get a copy of *The Little Engine That Could* for Chanukah from Aunt Esther and think that she spent $200 on it? Warman hated price clipped books, and although many of his better books were thus afflicted, he generally reduced his prices accordingly. He ran his shop pretty much by the book.

By this time, I had become thoroughly immersed in learning all I could about books, and especially about first editions and how to identify them. I had become a habitué of most of the local used booksellers on an almost daily basis, and had developed a regular route which took me to Mesa, Tempe and to downtown Phoenix where there were a couple of pretty decent shops on Camelback Road. I seemed to become mesmerized when confronted with a nice copy of a good book. Powerless over this bizarre affliction, I bought book after book after book.

The depths of my contagion grew worse. My wife began to carp and complain incessantly. She had initially supported my enthusiasm and had even accompanied me on some of my early booking binges. She had jokingly talked about inventing a "book muzzle" for people who, like myself, were simply unable to restrain themselves. But she soon began to tire of my excesses. As our funds began to diminish, I harangued her about wasting money on frivolities such as food, clothing and medication. The diminution in our bank account was matched by a rapid increase in the number of stacks of books which littered our entire house. Typically, I would return from a day's booking with one or more of those flimsy plastic sacks containing the day's catch. It generally varied from six to thirty volumes, and I would immediately stack these treasures on the night stand next to my side of the bed so I could theoretically "start reading them right away." Of course in so doing, I would be forced to move the previous day's material to some other spot, not too far from the night stand.

Well, as you can guess, I never actually was able to read more than a small fraction of what I had purchased, and before long there were small piles and large piles all over the house. And I mean all over. They were in the bedroom, in the kitchen and in the closets. Like kudzu, the piles spread and grew taller until they covered virtually every square foot of our home, and had begun to creep out into the garage. The car was filled, with the passenger's side inaccessible. Books on the car floor, in the trunk and over-flowing the back seat. And still I continued to bring more and more books home. I was helpless in the face of this addiction. I had become possessed.

My local sources soon became inadequate. Unable to slake the unquenchable thirst of my lust with the material that surfaced here in the Phoenix area, I began to drive long distances to bookshops in San Diego, Los Angeles, Denver and San Francisco. Suddenly, and with no plan-ning or preparation, I would find myself barreling west on Interstate 10, making the twelve hour round-trip drive to San Diego for a mere four or five hours worth of browsing the many shops which were to be found on Adams Avenue. And of course Wahrenbrock's and a few others downtown. And then, after perhaps a side trip up to Acacia Avenue Books in Solana Beach, I would simply do a U-ee and drive back to Phoenix. A fifteen or twenty hour excursion. Always with some newly acquired books.

The 1700 mile round-trip drive to San Francisco up Route 5 became a monthly event. It was a grueling drive, but I was spurred on by the adrenaline rush occasioned by the very thought of spending five or six hours scrounging around at Serendipity Books in Berkeley.

A huge two-story operation, Serendipity **had the books**. At prices which were generally about fifty percent higher than anywhere else in the Western Hemisphere, but a marvelous selection. The owner, a strange fellow burdened by an irrational, almost feeble-minded devotion to the hapless San Francisco Giants baseball team, probably

knew as much about modern literature and fiction as anyone I had ever met. And, with a keen sense of *noblesse
oblige* he was generally willing to share some of this vast
wellspring of knowledge with his customers and visitors.
Especially if the Giants had won the night before. And
more especially if the Dodgers had lost. I actually began to
follow the two teams on the radio in the Lincoln, and when
I learned that the Giants were in the process of beating the
Dodgers in a head-to-head contest (a rare enough occur-
rence), I would set out immediately for the Bay Area so as
to capitalize on the festive mood which, certain to last only
until the next game, would often result in some relatively
good buys at Serendipity. On one occasion, the Giants had
been leading the Dodgers by a score of 7 to 2 in the eighth
inning. I had almost reached Modesto when I heard the
Dodgers come up with six runs in the top of the eighth to
win the game 8 to 7. As Dodger announcer Vin Scully jubi-
lantly described the Giants last out, I numbly cut across the
median and headed back down south to Phoenix.

While in The People's Republic of Berkeley, I would
always try to hit Moe's Books and Black Oak Books, both
near the fabled University of California at Berkeley cam-
pus, with its carnival-like ambience and world class
mélange of stupefied junkies, bikers with pierced tongues
and scrotums, hookers with pierced lips and nipples,
freaks with spiky purple hair, dreadlocked whackos, and
skinheads with full body tattoos, almost all of whom were
working on their Ph.D.s in molecular astrophysics or
behavioral science.

Because of the length of the drive to San Francisco, I
always overnighted. My second day was usually spent in
the Mission District, where a number of small but excellent booksellers had inexplicably located their opera-
tions. Tall Stories, smack in the middle of the Mission, a

collective with about fifteen dealers exhibiting under the same roof, was always fertile territory. Taking special care not to trip over, or otherwise disturb the many denizens of the area who sprawled in drunken or drug induced stupors on the sidewalks, or who were busily shooting-up, fornicating or moving their bowels in the shallow doorways of the many colorful storefronts, I lurched from shop to shop. From Bolerium Books to Carroll's Books to Adobe Books on 16th Street. Anxious not to allow even a single treasure to escape my detection and ultimate possession.

Even Denver was not too great a distance for my diseased mind to carry me. Not really a great booktown, I still made infrequent visits to Tattered Cover Books and to Kugelman & Bent on Colfax. Both were decent shops, and run by OK people. And of course, how could I possibly afford to miss the Old Algonquin Bookstore? This place was owned and operated by a guy named John Dunning, who had himself written a pretty successful murder mystery about rare books and used book dealers. Published by Scribners in 1992 at a retail price of $19.95, the first printing had been quite small, and within a few months the book was bringing as much as $150. I think that about ninety-nine percent of the rare bookdealers in North America had been to Old Algonquin trying to get Dunning to sign or inscribe their first editions of *Booked to Die.* He was an obliging kind of character, and rarely turned down such a request. And no trip to Denver would have been complete without a stop at Stage House II Books in Boulder, about a half hour drive from Denver. And Rue Morgue Books selling only books dealing with murder and mayhem. I occasionally found a good deal there. Like first editions of Charles

Willeford's gritty *Miami Blues* and *Kiss Your Ass Goodbye.* A steal at $110 for the pair.

Always staying in fleabag motels and eating at cheap luncheonettes and dilapidated beaneries, I tried to stretch my meager financial reserves, but it soon became apparent that the costs of the travel were becoming unmanageable and cutting into the funds available for the acquisition of yet more books. So, I began to purchase books from out of town dealers by telephone, by fax, and by mail.

I had for some months been a subscriber to *AB Bookman's,* a weekly trade journal for the used and rare book trade. Advertisements for books wanted and for books offered for sale appeared in each issue. It didn't take me long to figure out that this thing was a complete waste of time and money. My copy arrived with mind-numbing regularity on Thursdays, and I would feverishly but methodically scour the Books For Sale columns, circling with red pen the books which I wanted to buy. Working at a frantic pace, I would dive to the phone, and start my series of as many as forty long-distance phone calls hoping to land some of these great finds. Time after time, and call after call, I was shut out. All of the bargains had already been garnered either by the magazine's staff, who saw the ads before the rest of the world, or by the sharpies from New York and other points east who received their copies of *AB* on Wednesdays. A day before mine arrived. These long-distance phone calls became not only another big expense, but an enormous source of aggravation as I was told, "Oh, sorry, that book was sold yesterday." Call after call. So, I never really had any kind of a chance to get anything much good, and I began to wonder why I, or anyone else west of the Mississippi, bothered to subscribe to this joke unless they would coordinate the mailings so as to give all of their readers a fighting chance.

One morning, having just been shot down by a dealer from Georgia with a hideous drawl who had advertised "a bright clean copy" of *The Love Nest* by Ring Lardner in an "equally bright dust jacket" at the incredibly low price of $40, I blew my cork and called *AB*'s offices in New York. I was told that the management was all tied up in meetings for the rest of the day, but that "someone would call me back." Of course nobody ever returned my call, but obviously somebody took some action. No longer did my *AB* come on Thursdays. Right. You guessed it. Fridays, with an occasional Saturday delivery thrown in for good measure. Like I said, a real waste of time.

So, next I got into buying from catalogs. I had ordered catalogs from a number of the major mail order dealers across the country and soon my mail box was stuffed with fresh catalogs on a daily basis. Ken Lopez Books from Massachusetts. Else Fine from Michigan. The Bookshelf, Jack's Book Stack, Waverly Books and Len Unger Rare Books, all out of Southern California. Joseph The Provider in Santa Barbara. Antic Hay and Between The Covers from New Jersey. Willis Herr and Mary Mason Books down in San Diego. I was receiving nearly thirty catalogs per week, and I was poring over them and ordering with both hands. And the books began to arrive. In crates and in cartons. In boxes and in padded envelopes. By mail, by Federal Express and by United Parcel Service. Packages large and small began to line up and stack up in my home. In the few spots not yet already covered by stacks of books. I couldn't even unpack them as fast as they arrived at my front door. All stuffed with excelsior, with shredded newspapers, with bubble wrap and with those horrible little styrofoam peanuts. My garbage service began to complain about the overfilled garbage containers-overflowing with cardboard cartons and the mountains of packing materials used to keep the books secure and free from damage.

But buying from catalogs wasn't the perfect solution either. These books were *expensive*. I don't mean a little expensive, I mean drop dead expensive. Not only did these dealers have good—no, great merchandise— they knew how to charge for it. It's not exactly that they overcharged, but there just weren't any bargains in the catalogs. You couldn't buy a $150 book for $15. And especially not from dealers like Ken Lopez or Joe The Pro. Those guys knew exactly what they had and wanted top prices for what were top quality books. I was going broke. And it was happening in a hurry.

My poor wife finally left me. I remember that it was on a Thursday morning when I saw her for the last time. Thursdays had been reserved for a swing through the nearly thirty Phoenix area bookstores which sold strictly new books. I would scavenge these stores in a search for treasures on the remainder tables. Never finding anything even remotely worth buying, I still found it impossible to resist buying tons of absolute dreck. And in larger and larger quantities. Like the day I discovered Darryl Brock's excellent baseball novel *If I Never Get Back* had been remaindered at Bookstar, and I bought all thirty-seven copies. Anyway, I was leaving the house at exactly 7:45 a.m. and I asked her to keep the blinds and draperies shut. I couldn't afford to have the sun touch my treasures. Sunning could, after all, fade the colors on the dust jackets. I guess that was the last straw for her. When I arrived home at my usual six o'clock that evening, I found her gone. Just a handwritten note:

*I think you have gone mad. You and your books
have driven me out. I can't take any more. I have
fixed some stir fry vegetables for you and there is
marinara sauce in the freezer. Try to eat. My attorney, Bernie Kornblum will contact you.*

*   P.S. Tim called from Mesa Books. He said he has
a nice copy of Mark Harris' Southpaw for $200. Also,
a dealer called from Santa Barbara. He said he had
a fine* Cunts *signed by John Updike. I hung up on
him before he could tell me the price. You should see
a psychiatrist.*

After all I had done for her. And *given* to her. Last May,
for our anniversary, *"B" is for Burglar* by Sue Grafton. A
nice signed copy which had cost me $375. And then in
November, for her birthday, a beautiful example of Peter
Beagle's *The Last Unicorn*. Not exactly chopped liver at
$125.

What the hell did she know anyhow, I told myself. I
remember actually being glad that she had gone. It meant
a little extra storage space. I carried in the twenty-four
copies of Nicholson Baker's *Room Temperature* which I
had scored at Brentano's at three bucks a pop, and carefully stacked them on her side of the bed. The disease was
progressing.

Unbelievably, I now began to expand even further the
scope of my forays. I was ready to strike out on my own
and start to uncover that fabulous El Dorado of rare books
at incredibly low prices which I knew existed somewhere
out there. Even though most of the used book stores had
treated me very well, and generally allowed me the standard twenty percent discount normally reserved for dealers, I was no longer able to afford to buy their books. I had
developed an interest in the works of Damon Runyon and

Ring Lardner, and had found that nice copies of books by these authors, with original dust jackets, ran up to $300 or $400 apiece. Between what I had been spending on books and losing at the polar bear races out at Turf Paradise on Sundays, when most used bookstores were closed, and what I jokingly called "my day off," I was lucky to be able to afford a wiener at Ted's Charcoal-Broiled Hots out on Broadway in Tempe for lunch. Where they actually flew their weenies in from Buffalo. So much for the Damon Runyon and Ring Lardner first editions.

So I started haunting thrift stores and antique shops in outlying areas where the "rubes" might not know the real value of any old books they might have. I began to cruise the seamy neighborhoods in Phoenix, Glendale and Mesa where there was a multiplicity of Goodwill and Salvation Army thrift shops. Humane Society, hospital, church and synagogue thrift shops. I was now finding myself sitting in the, by this time battered and decrepit Lincoln, with the engine running, on Van Buren Street in downtown Phoenix at seven o'clock in the morning sucking on a styrofoam cup of coffee and glumly munching a greasy sugar donut while waiting for my new hangouts to open their doors. Temple Shalom Thrift Shop or Hezbollah Arm The Arabs Thrift Shop. It didn't matter at all. I lined up with the nameless, ragged and toothless, standing on sidewalks littered with empty pint bottles of Ripple and Thunderbird, and blanketed with crushed soft drink containers, Big Mac wrappers and other Mactrash. Eager to enter these grimy and gritty grottos. They, I told myself, *needed* to be here. To buy the essentials of life. I, on the other hand, was here by choice—slumming in a fashion, seeking rare books. Just remembering the countless fruitless hours I spent in those fetid, dimly-lighted dungeons, crawling around on hopelessly filthy floors and squinting at books which were either placed on shelves too high to be visible or too low to inspect without lying flat on my side, makes me nauseous. Creeping along like an infantryman on my stomach, through piles of smelly discarded clothing and shoes. The pox had brought me to my knees. Literally. And yet it would get worse. Much worse.

How can I expect you to understand the depravity and dementia which had me so firmly in its grasp? I felt myself being sucked into a dangerous undertow and trying to extricate myself. Never again, I would say to myself after each unrewarded excursion. But I couldn't get out. Couldn't stop. I found just enough to keep me convinced that I was only one stop from the Holy Grail. My best find from these thrifts, cluttered with used wooden salad tongs, chipped, fake Fiestaware dishes, African tribal masks carved from coconut husks in The Philippines and paintings of bullfight scenes on black velvet, was a copy of Tim O'Brien's *If I Die in a Combat Zone*. It was in mediocre condition, with a badly chipped dust jacket, and inscribed by some idiot to her boyfriend on the front free end paper. It was a lengthy and impossibly stupid message "To Harold," and was written in ink. There forever. While an inscription or signature by a book's author always increases the value of a book, inscriptions by former owners are most undesirable. Mutilations. Having no interest in Vietnam war literature, and needing any cash I could lay my hands on, I quickly sold it to Lenny for $75. If the dust jacket had been a little nicer, and had there not been that insipid inscription, I could have gotten $200 or $250 for it. I had paid one buck at St. Vincent DePaul's out in Peoria.

I had by now abandoned all pretense of normalcy. I had even discontinued my once a week excursion to the track, and soon lost all contact with any friends I had left.

Formerly gregarious and extroverted, I could no longer afford the time to maintain even the most cursory social connections. Regular meals had all but vanished from my diseased memory.

I dined on snacks and junk food. On the fly. As I drove maniacally from bookstore to antique shop to junk store. And, in the few waking hours which I actually spent at home, I pored over research material in a relentless effort to learn more about these books which had become the essence of my very existence.

Was it a true first edition? If so, was it the first state? I developed a penchant for minutiae befitting the madman I had become. I had learned for example, that Steinbeck's *Cannery Row* had been bound with a buff-colored cloth, and that, partially through the printing of the first edition, they had run short and switched to a canary yellow cloth. Thus, while both the buff and yellow were true first editions, the buff was the "first state" and thus of greater value to collectors. I learned who had done the artwork on a number of especially good dust jackets. I could almost name them all from memory regardless of their obscurity. I had developed a knowledge of bindings and paper quality. Of print and typesetting. Of textures and smells. Yes, smells. I would frequently sniff a book to see if it had been the property of a smoker. I could practically tell you what brand he smoked after just a cursory whiff. And "points." Were there any points? Those little totally innocuous, barely perceptible signs which distinguish a "true first" from a second state of a first edition? Like the extra line of type on page 270 of Jerzy Kosinski's *Painted Bird*. The detailed concerns of a warped and perverted mind.

And then, I began my final descent. My ultimate degradation. The very road to my own private hell. I began to attend garage sales. Garage sales, yard sales, patio sales, carport sales, basement sales, estate sales, moving sales, multifamily sales, neighborhood sales and benefit sales. Sales to benefit cats and sales to benefit dogs. Sales for nurses, hospitals, Temples and Churches, libraries and soccer leagues. Sales for policemen and firemen. Sales for Boy Scouts, Girl Scouts, Cub Scouts and Brownies. Sales for the deaf, the blind, the lame and the halt. Sales for the Rotary, the Kiwanis, the Elks, the Lions and the Moose. And they all had books.

These sales took place for the most part on Saturdays and Sundays. Many were advertised in the morning paper, and some were found by merely driving around. The sales were indicated by signs, usually crudely fashioned, which were on virtually every corner. Most done on shocking-pink, day-glo orange, or neon-chartreuse cardboard. With arrows pointing the way to the sale.

And what sales they were. A mind boggling array of trash. That human beings could ever have owned such abominable furniture and fixtures was almost unthinkable. And discarded clothing which would have been rejected by every beggar in Calcutta. All offered for sale. And now the books. Books? Well, almost. I mean, they were books inasmuch as they had covers and pages with words on them. But books? Not really.

I have neither the time left nor the inclination to give you a complete education in booking, but I'll try to give you a basic rundown of what was to be found at these garage sales, and how it bore little resemblance to anything I was looking for. First, there were the paperbacks. To me, a paperback was a paperback. I soon learned that to these garage sale people, paperbacks were considered books. An ad in the *Arizona Republic* would describe a garage sale featuring "lots of books." I'd frantically drive the forty miles out to Ahwatukee, only to find two hundred paperbacks. Not books. **Paperbacks.** Worthless.

Next on the parade of horrors comes something which makes paperbacks look like the crown jewels. These little gems are Reader's Digest Condensed Books, or any other condensation. Good only for kindling on a chilly night, or sooner. At least the paperbacks have the entire text. Of equal value are self-help books. Books with titles like *Creative Aggression, Pulling Your Own Strings, Earning Money Without a Job* and *Life 101*. Also worthless are books which describe how to use a computer, go through menopause or grow vegetables. And these showed up by the hundreds of thousands at garage sales. One more copy of Gail Sheehy's *Passages*, and I would have started to scream. Also the ubiquitous out-of-date management books, found in abundance especially like *The One Minute Manager*. These dandy items abounded in upscale or yuppie neighborhoods. Genuine atrocities; worth zilch.

Then, there are the millions of books about how to raise your children without ever having to see them, banal biographies about fatuous movie stars, political personalities and vapid princes of commerce like Iacocca and Donald Trump. Then come the zillions of ripped, blasted and crayoled kid's books. Which are invariably recent reprints of older ripped, blasted and crayoled kid's books. How these citizens had the nerve to display this shit in public I'll never know.

I've already gone into the Book of The Month Club routine. Absolutely astounding how much of this chazerai existed out there. And of course sometimes they look so much like the real thing, that you actually have to touch one before you know. Yech! They actually feel different. Lighter in overall weight than a real book, the dust jackets on BOMC material are from an inferior paper stock, and the lack of varnish on the paper makes them feel sort of chalky to the touch. They spared no expense to cut costs on this junk. At least the other refuse was never intended to fool anybody. But the BOMCs? Bogus! Fakes, phonies, frauds and counterfeits.

So, that's the basic scenario. First, eliminate the paperbacks. Next, separate the condensed stuff and the BOMC material. Forget about all the biography, self-help, management, kid's junk and the like. And if there is anything left, then you can first start to look and see if it's a first edition. Not to mention the fact that, even if it is, you can skip all of the big name, popular authors. Danielle Steel, Jackie Collins, Sidney Shelton and so on. Their books aren't worth collecting, not only for lack of literary merit, but because they are printed by the trainload, and can be found for sale at Price Club and every other discount emporium in the Western Hemisphere. More trash. I guess that by now you get the picture. Finding anything worthwhile is like looking for a needle in five haystacks. Maybe harder. Yet, insanity is all one needs to prod him along from one junk sale to the next. A little craziness goes a long way.

The morning of April 16th got off to a bad start. Saturday. Garage sale day. I woke at my customary 6:00 A.M. with visions of Edward Abbeys and Larry McMurtrys dancing in my head. Would this be the day? Would I stumble across a couple of Hammetts or Hemingways? Maybe a nice first edition of *A Time To Kill* by John Grisham, author of *The Firm.* This book, his first, wasn't any better than his next few, and even though it had been published in 1989 was unbelievably already bringing as much as $2500. First to the newspaper. The classifieds. Where were the sales offering BOOKS? I needed to establish which sector of the vast Phoenix metropolitan area I would tackle this morning. So much to do. So little time. My eyes hit the sports page, and I was shocked to read the headline that Joe Montana was going to become the next Phoenix Cardinal quarterback. Not that I followed sports anymore. I had dropped my interest in baseball and football along with all of my other normal pursuits. But **Joe Montana**. I had made a career out of hating this guy. From way back when he was a rat-faced quarterback for the fighting Irish of Notre Dame. Fighting Irish all right. A bunch of Wops and Polacks who annually led the nation in penalties for unnecessary roughness and unsportsmanlike conduct. I hated him while I lived in the Bay Area and he quarterbacked for the Forty Niners. What a bunch of smug, egocentric bastards. And now he was coming here. Was this putz following me? My stomach growled and I ate a couple of Hostess cupcakes for breakfast. Not the chocolate ones. The orange ones looked a lot healthier. With a microwaved cup of instant coffee. Black. I had run out of both sugar and Mocha Mix. It was an omen. A bad omen.

Part 2
THE INCIDENT

A s I said, the day was to get worse. I had decided to concentrate my efforts up near my home, in northern Phoenix and Scottsdale. I'm not certain why, but none of the ads jumped out at me. So I figured that by not involving myself in a long trek I might be able to cover an extra six or seven stops. I headed out.

The first three sales were uneventful as usual. The same junk. With frowzy, sleepy-looking hausfraus sitting watch from the shade of their open garages. Some still in their housecoats and slippers. A few with rollers in their hair. It was best not to look at them too directly. Just take a quick visual survey and slink away. By averting the eyes, one didn't have to bother exchanging pleasantries, or listen to their inane drivel about the superlative quality of what you had already noted was some subhuman third world dreck. The lady at stop number three asked loudly, "See anything you can use?" But I had already started skulking back to the Lincoln, and just kept going.

It was at my fourth stop that I should have known that it wasn't going to be my day. It was about eight A.M. and as I rolled up to a row of cookie-cutter, stuccoed, frame homes with red tiled roofs just off of 39th St., I did a double take. Parked directly across the street from me was a light metallic blue van. A Dodge. I knew that van. Oh God, I silently prayed, don't let it be! But it was. Yes, it was. George Nestor. NO! NO! NO! Not Nestor. But it *was*

George, and his broad grin was enough to tell me that I had missed something good. He was loading a carton into the van, and had two more on his hand-dolly next to the curb.

"Hey, man, how ya doin'," he shouted. "Come 'ere and take a gander at these."

George Nestor was a partner in one of the used book shops on Camelback Road. I think I mentioned them earlier. He was a little weird but generally good-natured and marginally knowledgeable. Thin and wiry, he had curly blond hair, bird-like features and moved with a hurky jerky series of robot-like maneuvers. My problem with Nestor was that he was a world-class book hound. If there was ever a decent sale anywhere in North America George Nestor would be first in line. One popular story about him which circulated for some time was that he was seen first in line at the Visiting Nurse's book sale, a very big annual event in Phoenix for which people actually begin lining up at two o'clock in the morning, and at the very same time he was spotted first in line at book sales in Pawtucket, Rhode Island, Altoona, Pennsylvania and Coxsackie, New York, a town renowned not only for the inevitable lewd and salacious allusions evoked by its name, but also for having the dubious distinction of being the only city on the planet which is namesake to a virus. Nestor had become a living legend. But this was a nothing little garage sale far removed from his normal territory. How in the hell had he sniffed this one? I felt my teeth grinding as I forced a smile and a cheery, "Mornin' George, how's it going?"

I meandered across to his van to check out his latest coup. Smiling all the way, I hoped the son of a bitch would get a heart attack in front of my eyes. I just couldn't stand it. Oh please God, let it be nonfiction. I mean I had had nightmares about this guy. In all of these bad dreams Nestor had beaten me to a major collection. The two car-

tons on the dolly were full of old pulp science fiction maga-
zines. From the late 1920s and early '30s. In beautiful condition too. He positively beamed. His eyes always seemed
to be spinning around in their tiny sockets. Even more so
this morning.

"That ain't nothin'," he gloated. "Take a look see here."
He bent over to open the box he had been trying to lift into
the van.

My worst nightmare come true. Books. Very good
books. I mean books like a first edition of Ann Rice's
Interview with the Vampire. In average condition. Worth
at least $300. A fine copy had recently sold at auction for
$650. And about fifty more good books. None as valuable
as *The Interview,* but one hell of a haul. I felt like vomiting.
"Nice find, George," I croaked. "But say, aren't you a little
far from home?"

"Aw, I guess not. Not really." He actually talked like
that. For a split second I thought he was going to say "Aw
shucks" and do a soft shoe shuffle. "I was just on my way
up to Flagstaff where I heard about a nice bunch of leather
bound books for sale, and I happened to see the sign for
this nice lady's sale." He nodded toward the wretched old
hag who was smiling at us as she sat in a beat-up wicker
rocking chair with a price tag on it. "Gawd," he said, "I
think these old sci fi mags are worth at least $50 each.
And," he added for good measure, "I guess there's at least a
hun'ert of 'em here." As if I couldn't count.

Nestor's estimate of $50 each for the science fiction stuff
was on the low side. I knew a dealer in upstate New York
who would give a kidney to be able to buy them at $80
each. And George had paid $35 for all three cartons.
Unfucking believable. I quickly calculated that he had
made a quick $13,000 or more. And I had missed it by ten
minutes. I sat in the Lincoln and literally shook like a leaf.

Nestor. The son of a bitch talked like Goofy and looked like Big Bird. Him and his goddamned partner LaVerne. I think she was a former stripper or porno star. The word was that she had supplied the cash. Nobody could figure out who supplied the brains.

Only half past eight and it was already like a blast furnace inside the Lincoln. The poor vehicle had, on at least ten occasions, been caught in the sporadic flurries of gunfire which erupt periodically among the many hot and sweaty but enthusiastic motorists trapped on the congested highways in and around Phoenix. While most of the damage sustained by the Lincoln had been run-of-the-mill—bullet pocked doors, fenders and trunk lid along with the customary fractured windshield—the air conditioner had taken a direct hit by an errant .30 caliber slug, and had long since given up the ghost, as had the radio and three of the power windows. I sat there behind the wheel, shaking, sweating and dazed. I felt like quitting for the day. I should have.

Muttering maledictions for Nestor, I revved the engine to a savage roar and squealed away from the curb. "Rotten old bitch," I snarled under my breath. The old woman smiled sweetly and wiggled her fingers at me in a sort of wave good-bye. She had no way of knowing the deep hatred I felt for her and for everyone else in the world at that moment.

I persisted. I seemed to be driving myself as a sort of punishment. I was sick of books, sick of Nestor, sick of sweating and sick to the bone of Arizona. Sick of garage sales and the crap these people were trying to unload. Like moldy old copies of *National Geographic* and Nancy Reagan's pissy autobiography. *My Turn.* Who cares. Zero. Zip.

Almost blindly I headed north on 40th St. and simply

drove on with no plan and no destination. I saw a few signs for sales, but the heart had gone out of me. I was through. I could no longer even function. I kept seeing Nestor's stupidly grinning face. I had passed Thunderbird Road, and was now out in the boonies. I saw a ground squirrel dash into the road, and I swerved trying to nail him, but he heard the Lincoln—which by now rattled and knocked like a clown car at the circus—dodged, and I missed him. I was sure that I saw him give me the finger as I sailed harmlessly by.

I turned right on Bell Road and drove numbly for another fifteen minutes or so. I had reached northern Scottsdale, and found myself at 110th St. A terrible area for booking, this was a new community with virtually all new homes. No old folk. Very few moving out, and little activity in general. I headed south. Sort of in the general direction of home. One whipped puppy. And then I saw the sign. Crudely hand-lettered on a piece of brown cardboard cut from an old carton. Estate sale. With an arrow. I followed the arrows to a cul-de-sac lined with typical cheap, stucco, tract houses. Each looked exactly like the other, and like a million homes all over this freaking state. Why bother stopping. There were two other cars parked out front. More junk. But I stopped anyway and got out of the car. My feet felt like lead and I had a terrible case of dry mouth. Summoning whatever force of will I had left, I casually trudged up the driveway to the card tables laden with the usual trash. A pair of massive, tarnished brass candelabras and an old ashtray from Hawaii circa 1945 and shaped like a pineapple were the feature items on table number one. A pair of plastic binoculars missing one of the lenses. A crutch. Jesus, a goddamn old crutch. I almost began to laugh. I was so sick of this . . . ***wait a minute!*** I stopped dead in my tracks. Suddenly paralyzed, I couldn't believe my eyes.

Under the next table. Table number two. Set up half in the driveway and half in the shade of the open garage. Cartons of books. Many cartons. Each carton had a hand written 4x6 card taped neatly to the side. Books $1 each. Six for $5. That was it. With the stealth of a leopard and the speed of a cheetah I was already kneeling next to the first box which was open at the top. My heart pounded and my temples throbbed. Right on top. My God! *The Big Sleep* by Raymond Chandler. But wait! There was something wrong. The book was new. An obvious reprint. Chandler's first book had been published in 1939. No way could this have been any older than a few years. It was perfect. And then I noticed that this book and the others in the carton had all had their dust jackets neatly enveloped in a protective cellophane-like material. Like book collectors use. Momentarily stunned, I tried to put the pieces together. I looked inside the book. ***It was indeed a first,*** the words FIRST EDITION boldly appearing on the copyright page! A perfectly preserved copy! Mint. No sunning on the spine. No tears or chips. A once in a lifetime find, a dream come true, a genuine, perfect copy of one of the most sought-after books in the world. A timeless classic. I knew that Ahearn's *Guide to Values of Collected Books* listed this book at $2500. But not Ahearn, nor anyone else for that matter, had ever seen a copy like this. With bright vivid colors. I had no idea of how this book had survived this way for more than a half century, but I knew how Balboa must have felt as he finally saw the Pacific Ocean. Or was it Magellan? I looked back to the box from which I had lifted out *The Big Sleep.*

Oh God, I thought I was going to die. This was not possible. More Chandlers: *The Lady in the Lake, Farewell My Lovely, The Little Sister, The Long Goodbye, The Smell of*

Fear. Each copy as magnificent as the first. These books were flawless. Each glistened beneath its protective plastic wrapper like a diamond freshly polished. What had I found? Clearly there had never been a collection in this condition unearthed before.

Agatha Christies were next. Seven separate volumes. Each again without flaw. Staggering, brilliant dust jackets. *The Man in the Brown Suit, Murder on the Orient Express . . . .* I was dazed. Chandler, then Christie. Had this been a fanatical collector of detective or mystery fiction? No! That was not it. The next volume was an absolutely pristine copy of Walter Van Tilburg Clark's *Ox Bow Incident*, published in 1940. Certainly not detective or mystery related. What *was* this? I wiped my eyes which by now were wildly blinking away the sweat which poured from my forehead. My hands were shaking so violently that I was almost afraid to pick up these priceless volumes.

The next book provided the answer. *The Hunt For Red October.* Published in 1984 by the Annapolis Press. An extremely small printing of this, Tom Clancy's first book, had made it an overnight rarity. The true first edition did not have a price on the dust jacket. And here it was. This book had been seen before in mint condition, and copies that nice had been selling for $800. But the key was in the authors' last names. Chandler, Christie, Clark, Clancy . . . . *I had found the "Cs"!* Oh Jesus. If this were the C box, and there were similar boxes for the rest of the alphabet I would soon own one of the finest collections of modern fiction in the world.

My mind whirled. Feverishly I began to calculate how many I would need to sell so as to stabilize my impoverished lifestyle, and so as to be able to keep the rest of my new library in secure surroundings befitting such a magnificent collection. Visions of rich, dark, rosewood paneling, teak and mahogany shelving, Tiffany shaded table lamps and luxuriant forest green leather-covered club chairs danced in my addled mind. I could almost hear the strains of Tchaikovsky's violin concerto in D minor wafting through this fantasy room as I jerked myself back to the reality of crawling around in this sweltering, spider infested garage and the deal I was about to consummate.

Meanwhile, I had slithered on my knees to the next box in line. This one just inside the open garage. Gently unfolding the flaps I saw that I had found box F. Faulkners. At least a dozen mint Faulkners. Priceless. For although no one had ever actually been able to read a Faulkner, his books were wildly sought by collectors everywhere. Ferber, Fitzgerald . . . .

"Can I help you?" I almost jumped out of my skin. There were two pink LA Gear running shoes standing next to me as I groveled helplessly on my hands and knees. Inside the LA Gears were two feet to which were attached a couple of stout legs. These belonged to the fortyish, chunky, bleached-blond standing, arms akimbo, with an amused smile on her face as she looked down at me.

"Huh?" I replied glibly. Desperately trying to recover my composure, but still staggered by the enormity of my find, I scrambled to my feet. "The books," I said. "The books." My voice sounded like I was talking underwater. I was struggling to get hold of myself. I wanted nothing more than to get these loaded in the Lincoln. I was certain that I would have to make at least three trips, and I cursed Nestor for his roomy Dodge van. I would have paid him anything for that van.

"Oh," she said. "Grandpa's old books. He was crazy for 'em."

"Yes, yes I see." was the best I could muster. "I, uh, like books too."

"Yes," she continued as if she hadn't heard me, "Grandpa passed on about four years back. He lived for those books. Granny, she never cared a fig for 'em. Me 'n' Eddie, he's my husband, we drug all those books clear out here from Sun City to hep Granny get rid of 'em."

Jesus, I thought, everybody out here talks like the god-damned Hatfields and McCoys. I tried to smile, but my left eye was twitching and I seemed to be going numb from the neck down. "The books. I'd like, uh, I want to buy the books." More snappy repartee.

"Oh yeah." she said. "How many you like?"

"Oh," I said slyly, then hesitated for effect, "I think I'll take about, uh, oh heck," I glanced down at my topsiders and tried to look sheepish. "I guess, uh, I think I'll take 'em all."

"All?" She looked at me in amazement. "But we got over eight hun'red books here. Mister, you're lookin' at an awful lot of money."

Eight hundred books! That's what she said. I felt giddy and lightheaded. Even at an average of $1000 per copy we were talking about nearly one million bucks. And I had seen books that could easily sell for $5000 or more! This collection was indeed priceless. A banged-up yellow Ford Taurus pulled up in front of the house next door, and two middle-aged Hispanic looking women got out and began to walk up the drive. A feeling of panic began to set in. I found it increasingly hard to breathe, let alone to talk.

"Books. I, uh, love books." I heard myself say. I tried to turn on my boyish charm. Which is particularly hard to do when you are in your mid-fifties, about thirty pounds over-weight, sweaty and unshaven. "I like, uh, love to read books."

"C'mon inside." She smiled. I felt the tension ease slightly as the Hispanic women slowly began to return to their auto. They had seen the cartons of books, but had shown absolutely no interest. I bent over and closed up the C box. I had already closed the Fs and the rest were still unopened.

Unwilling to leave the books for even a minute, I tried to decline her invitation politely and responded with my newly acquired élan and savoir faire. "Uh, uh, naw, uh, no thanks, it's OK, I'll uh, just pay you and uh . . . ."

She interrupted. "No, you *have* to come on inside. Granny's in there, and she wan'sa sell them books herself."

I was almost insane with lust, avarice and stark terror; visions of those blazing bright dust jackets were flashing on and off. It was like being on the strip in Vegas on New Year's Eve. Strangely, I began to wonder whether or not there was a mint copy of *The Postman Always Rings Twice.* By James Cain, 1934. After all, I hadn't yet gone through all the Cs.

Giddy now, almost in a blind stupor, I followed her through the garage and into the house. To deal with Granny. I glanced back over my shoulder at the boxes. A red Chevy Blazer came around the corner and cruised slowly by the house. Not seeing any firearms, medieval torture devices or anything else that appealed, the three young occupants screamed "Fuck ya'll" in unison, cranked up their stereo to mach four, speeded up and squealed their tires as they left the cul-de-sac. The screen door slammed shut behind me.

I followed her through the small but spotless kitchen, down a short narrow hallway carpeted with a seafoam-green spaghetti shag and into the living room.

"Say hello to Granny," she sang it like a little song. "Say hello to Granny."

"Hello Granny." I sort of hunched over as if trying to escape from the inanity of the whole experience. Granny, who looked as if she might have personally known Ben Franklin, actually leaped out of her easy chair and grasped my hand in a virtual death grip.

"Glad ta mee'cha young feller. You like books too?" Young feller? How had she known I was there for the books? And what did she mean **too?** A chill passed through me.

Granny spoke again. "Say hello to the Murdochs. *They* like books too."

I turned slowly as if suspended in a sea of molasses.

And then I saw them. Three of them. The Murdochs. Seated on the sofa under the front picture window. They seemed to nod at me in unison. None got up to shake my stupidly extended and by now rigid right arm. None smiled. The Murdochs. No one had said a word about books, but instinctively I knew that the Murdochs represented a problem. A big problem.

Two women and one man. All in the range of fifty-five to sixty-five. All nicely dressed. Mr. Murdoch had on a light tan Palm Beach suit, and wore a four-in-hand striped blue and yellow necktie. In Arizona. I don't recall ever having seen anyone wear a tie before in this state. Strange what one notices when the danger alarm goes off. He was almost bald, with just a fringe of white hair around the sides. Rimless glasses and white woven basket shoes. He looked like a plump, dapper version of the white rabbit from *Alice in Wonderland.*

As I would learn later, the two women were Mrs. Iris Murdoch, his wife, and Ms. Murdoch. Ms. Evelyn Murdoch. His sister.

"Man's come to buy your books Grams, says he wants to take 'em all," chirped my hostess. "Bet you didn't think so many folks would like your darn ol' books." Everything she said to grandma seemed to be sung to the tune of "Old

McDonald Had a Farm." "Eddie and I tol' ya, folks out here just love ta read."

Granny clucked a few times, and said, "Well mister, I think maybe you got here just a mite too late. These are the Murdochs, and, oh, I already tol' ya." She chortled as if charmed by her own stupidity. "And they've been here about fifteen minutes already—trying to get them books off of me."

I noticed that my hand was still extended although not to anyone in particular. I had just been holding it out in front of me as if trying to hitch a ride. I gasped. So they hadn't made a deal yet. The books were still up for grabs. I started to try to speak, to say something, when Mrs. Murdoch, Mrs. Iris Murdoch the wife, piped up.

"Well, Mrs. Deutch, you drive a hard bargain, but we'll take them." With that, she stood up and reached into her small pearled handbag. She withdrew a checkbook. Walking smartly to the Ethan Allen dining table across to the left, she seated herself and began to write. "Five hundred dollars, to Mrs. A. Deutch. April the sixteenth." She narrated the check as she wrote it.

"They was tryin' to get them books for $400," cackled the old woman. "I knowed they was worth mor'n 50¢ apiece." I tried to lower my outstretched arm since it appeared that nobody was about to shake with me, but oddly was unable to do so. I could feel the blood rushing to my feet, and was certain that I had suffered either a stroke or some type of siezure.

The room was spinning around. "Evan, you go get the car, and start loading up. Evelyn, give him some help. I'll be right out." The other two Murdochs, as though on cue, sprang into action. She turned to the old woman and touched her softly on the shoulder. Smiling warmly, and without missing a beat she kept up her incessant patter.

"Mrs. Deutch has a few other little things I'd like to pick up while we're out here. Can you come outside with me for a minute my dear?"

She was trying to get the old lady away from me! Get the car? Load up? Load up **my** books? I stood there swaying helplessly from side to side. I could not lose these books. Evan and Evelyn Murdoch had dutifully arisen from the sofa and headed out through the screen door into the garage. The man walked with a cane and had a pronounced limp. Iris Murdoch gently took old Mrs. Deutch by the arm, like a long lost friend, and started to guide her along to the garage. She never stopped talking all the time. "Lovely candelabras. Where in the world did you find them dear? How proud you must be of your charming granddaughter. What did you say her name was? Where exactly did you live in Milwaukee?"

I tried to think. I tried to speak. I could do neither. A low moaning noise seemed to be coming from my throat. The granddaughter, Louisa, turned to me. "Gee, how exciting. I can't imagine ever'one wanting them books, and all at once too. They didn't really seem all that in'erested 'fore you showed up." No longer able to stand, I sank into the easy chair formerly occupied by the old woman. *I was not going to let those books get away.* I knew that I had to act. Right away. My mind was numb. What could I do? What could I say? Louisa was looking at me with a sympathetic expression. She was my only hope. The batty old lady was impossible, and the Murdochs were clearly experienced and savage garage sale buyers. They had squashed me like a bug. Their whole routine had been a work of art. Almost like it had been choreographed by Busby Berkeley.

I spoke. "Please, uh please, I, I really need, uh, to have those books. Books. I love books." Any aplomb I had ever possessed had abandoned me. I was talking, but I wasn't saying anything. I felt like one of those cartoon characters. You know, like the cat trying to catch the mouse. Legs spinning in a giant circle, yet not moving. Unable to get traction. I heard a car outside, and glanced out the window.

It was a Cadillac. White, with ersatz gold trim and one of those horrible faux-convertible tops. Navy blue canvas. And it had Illinois plates. Evan Murdoch had swung the door open and was just emerging from the driver's side. Evelyn was already out. The car had been backed into the driveway, and sat at an angle with its front wheels on the street. Evelyn was moving toward the trunk, and Iris was holding one of the oversized brass candle holders which I had seen on table number one. Her mouth was moving and she appeared to be continuing to talk to old Mrs. Deutch.

This was it. No time for dreideling around. I felt myself coming together, and although my heart was still pounding wildly, I knew that I had to make my move. "More! I'll pay you more! I, I'm a student, no, a, uh, a teacher. My students need to have books." That's it I thought. The old poor students routine. I could almost picture a classroom filled with nine year olds, each reading a copy of Cormac McCarthy's *Child of God*. Yes, that was it! *Child of God*. A novel which, as the dust jacket proudly proclaimed, "explores the limits of human degradation." Necrophilia. *Child of God*. Child! God! That was it. God! I had seen the enormous family Bible on the credenza behind the dining table where Mrs. Murdoch had written the check. These people had religion. Probably Lutherans. My stupor had passed, and my thoughts were starting to gel. "Religion, I, I, uh, teach religion. My students, uh, they study religion. The books, uh, would be a big help. We **need** them."

Evelyn had the trunk open now, and I could see

Murdoch bending over and lifting a carton. "Yes, yes, religious school. Kids, uh, kids, need books." Panicked by the speed with which Murdoch was piling boxes into the cavernous trunk, I talked faster and faster.

"Pay more? How much more?" Her eyes had narrowed and bored into me. She hadn't heard a word I had said. Not about the kids, not about the religious school. Only my feeble offer to pay more money. I could see that Evelyn was loading a carton into the Caddy's back seat.

"A thousand! No, not a thousand, a thousand **more**! Fifteen hundred, maybe, uh, sixteen." I was babbling now. I realized the desperation of this game. I had to eliminate the Murdochs, yet I had to avoid at all costs letting on to the real worth of this treasure. To so do could alert them to what they were sitting on, and invite unbeatable offers from legitimate, solvent dealers. But the issue at hand was the Murdochs. They were really moving now, and I began to head toward the garage. The books were slipping away. I couldn't allow it.

"Did you say two thousand?" I whirled around. Louisa stared at me. Gone was the cheerful sparkle from her eyes. She stood once again with her hands on her hips, legs like tree trunks in her short, white, tennis skirt.

"Yes! Yes, I do! I did! Two thousand. I did say that. I said two thousand." My hand was pushing open the screen door, and I was stepping out into the garage. Louisa sprang into action and blasted by me like a shot.

Back out in the garage now, I sized up the situation at once. The trunk had been closed. The back seat of the Caddy was loaded with cartons, and Evelyn was seated in the front passenger's space. Murdoch was behind the wheel. Unbelievably, they had stacked up about ten or fifteen cartons near the curb, but a few feet to the right of the driveway. On the next door neighbor's property! *They knew! They knew!* They had not been able to fit all of the books into the car, but had effectively removed them from the old lady's possession. *They knew!* Iris stood next to the stacked cartons, clutching the pair of candelabras. She had a scowl on her face. She looked like she meant business. But then, so did I.

"Grams, Grams," I heard Louisa speaking to the old lady. "This man says that he'll pay more. He said two thou . . . ."

"Never you mind that now honey. A deal's a deal. These nice folk live outside Chicago now, but Iris here, she was original' from Milwaukee." Iris? They were already on a first name basis? Like old friends? Enraged by this cunning trio who had played old Mrs. Deutch like a fiddle, I sprinted down the driveway, across the gravelled front yard and jumped into the Lincoln. Furiously twisting the key in the ignition, I started it and rammed it into drive in one fluid motion. It surged forward, and I slammed on the brakes bringing it to a screeching, tire-smoking stop perpendicular to, and just inches in front of, Murdoch's Cadillac. I had him trapped. He was going nowhere. Not with **my** books he wasn't.

Jumping from the Lincoln, with its engine still running, I approached Iris who maintained her protective posture near the stacked cartons. She was only a few feet from the right front fender of the Caddy. "Listen, please, uh, just listen for a second." I tried to open some dialogue. My mouth was dry and my tongue felt like I had been eating a mixture of pickled herring and peanut butter.

"No, **you** listen!" she hissed. Both front doors opened simultaneously, as Murdoch and his slimy sister began to get out. I could see the plush maroon leather. Both were slightly overweight and, despite his limp, Murdoch and Evelyn were moving with unexpected speed and vigor.

"These are our property. Get your car away from us.

You, you . . . ." She was struggling. Searching for the right word. "Lowlife!" She had found it. Lowlife! This thieving bitch was calling me a lowlife. Evelyn had come up beside her, as if in support. I stared at them.

Murdoch came huffing and hobbling up. "Call the police," he shrieked to the old lady. He had made his pudgy little hands into fists, and held them in front of him à la Jack Johnson. He was trembling violently. So was I.

Iris approached me until her face was only inches from my own. She smelled faintly garlicky. "You vulgar son of a bitch," she whispered, "I'll show you who you're fucking with."

"Fucking with?" Had she really said that? I mean this woman looked like a country minister's wife. Prim. Proper. She wore a light-lavender, floral-print summer dress. A gauzy peach-colored scarf around her neck. Pillbox hat. The kind you don't see anymore. She glared at me through eyes which had narrowed to mere slits behind her fashionable bifocals. "**You** are scum." She enunciated clearly and deliberately.

She turned around, and grabbed at one of the cartons stacked behind her. Viciously yanking on the flaps, she grabbed a book. The violence of her movements caused several volumes to fall to the ground. *Fahrenheit 451.* Ray Bradbury, 1953. It fell onto the sidewalk and came to rest in an open position with the pages down. I noticed that the book had no dust jacket, then realized that it was one of only two hundred copies of this science fiction masterpiece which had been specially bound with asbestos boards instead of cloth binding, and signed by Bradbury. Virtually priceless. Several others fell apparently unharmed and landed on the cement portion of the driveway, next to the Caddy. I don't remember what they were, but I knew that she had found box B. Murdoch still stood in his caricature of a boxing stance. He was just to the right of his wife, and slightly behind her. "Police," he sniveled, "Call them please. Somebody help us."

By this time, some of the neighbors had come out to see what was doing. Small clusters of people were gathering here and there. A couple of little kids on tricycles were gaping at the scene from about four or five doors away. One of them, a girl of about five, was crying and yelling for her daddy. Shaking, and nearly comatose from fear and rage, I decided that I also would seek help. I too began to yell for the police. The situation was heading out of control.

"Bastard!" More profanities from Iris who had totally lost it. She ground her heel into the back of the flayed Bradbury, cracking the asbestos front panel and grinding the pristine white pages into the rough concrete of the sidewalk. In seconds she had reduced this irreplaceable treasure to rubble. Again she whirled. This time she knocked over the entire box, causing its contents to spill out onto the sidewalk and driveway. And then she did it.

Bending down, Iris, now beyond any semblance of control scooped up several books. "Slob! Asshole! Worthless scum!" She continued to curse me as she threw books hither and yon. Then, left holding only one book, she began to tear out the pages, crumple them and throw them in my face. To my horror, I saw that it was Thomas Berger's first novel. *Crazy in Berlin.*

How could she have known? How could anyone have known? Thomas Berger. The author of eighteen novels including *Little Big Man.* I idolized this man and his entire oeuvre. Witty and sophisticated, Berger's elegant use of the English language was extraordinary. Without exception, his books had received universal acclaim from reviewers and critics. I had even written to him on several occasions. I owned a nice first edition of every one of his books.

Except *Crazy*. It was a book of great scarcity. Every year or two a copy would turn up at auction or in one of the hundreds of catalogs to which I subscribed, but these copies were invariably in relatively poor condition. Mr. Berger himself, a reclusive type, had in response to one of my fan letters to him, written to me and explained that only about twelve hundred copies of *Crazy in Berlin* had actually been bound by the publisher, Scribners, in 1958.

And here it was, the finest copy extant. With its deep khaki and scarlet dust jacket. My own personal icon. Being shredded by a madwoman as I stood in helpless shock. It was too much. Can you understand? Have you ever just gone over the edge? I lunged for the book and tried to seize it from her. She had some strength for a person her size. We wrestled around for a few seconds until, with a Herculean heave, I pulled the book from her and flung her away from me. Evelyn had left the passenger's door open on the Caddy, and the force of my final desperate push propelled Iris directly into it. Stumbling backward, with wildly windmilling arms, the nape of her neck struck the cruelly sharp corner at the top of the open door with a sickening thud. She sagged, shuddered and slumped to the pavement.

Unintentional as my act of violence had been, I was horrified by the result. I stared at her body which lay face up and with arms outstretched. Her eyeglasses had broken and were attached at only one ear. Her dress was up over her knees. A small pool of blood had begun to form beneath her neck and shoulders and was trickling down the drive. I saw Louisa standing about fifteen feet away. She was holding her face with the palms of her hands and appeared to be screaming, although I don't remember hearing anything other than the sound of my own heart pounding furiously, and a drumming noise coming from the general direction of my temples. The old lady was nowhere to be seen.

Wham! Evelyn had come up behind me and smashed me with one of the brass candelabras. She had aimed at my head, but caught me on the right shoulder. The force of the blow knocked me down, and from the corner of my eye I saw that Murdoch himself had taken up the other candleholder and was limping toward me swinging wildly. I rolled away from him, and wobbled to my feet. I steadied myself with my left hand on the Caddy's rear fender and, summoning whatever remaining strength I had left, I dove for Evelyn and planted my head firmly into her stomach. She let out a terrific grunt and went down. As she fell backwards I managed to grab the bludgeon from her, and brought it crashing into the side of her head. A loud moan and she was still. I turned looking for Murdoch, half expecting his onslaught. Gone! Gone?

The Cadillac engine roared to life. That slime Murdoch had slipped behind the wheel while I had been dealing with his wife and sister, and was trying to flee. His exit was blocked by the still idling Lincoln, which by this time had begun to overheat and steam. He jammed the Caddy into reverse and careened backwards. Wildly trying to steer, he angled off to the left and neatly veered directly into the flagstone garage-facing. Quite accidentally he had hit Louisa and crushed her between the car and the wall. Probably unaware of what he had done, he slammed it into drive and fishtailed across the red-graveled front yard. Momentarily losing control or misjudging his route, the Caddy's right front fender blasted broadside into the Lincoln.

In retrospect, the whole episode sounds like a scene from a bad movie. A dark comedy. But this is exactly what happened. The force from the Cadillac's collision had apparently caused the Lincoln's transmission to slip from park into drive and, with steam pouring from under the hood, it ponderously began to travel on its own, headed toward the end of the cul-de-sac.

Meanwhile, the force of the crash into the massive Lincoln had been too much for the Caddy which had stalled out and sat motionless in the street. Murdoch ground mercilessly on the ignition. The engine wouldn't catch, but the feckless, frenetic grinding caused the fan blades to clatter against the mangled radiator. Like some horrible rap music, the sound of those blades beating spasmodically against the crumpled metal drove me to greater insanity. By now the Lincoln had lodged itself firmly against the entryway to the last house in the circle and, having taken out a huge saguaro cactus, had itself come to rest. Smoking, steaming and throbbing, it finally shuddered and died.

I made for Murdoch. I don't remember what I was thinking at the time. I knew that my life had in all likelihood come to a screeching halt, and I blamed Murdoch. He was, after all, the only one left. I grabbed the candelabra, which had rolled to the curb, and went for him. Seeing me approaching, Murdoch predictably moved quickly to lock the door. Grinding away on the ignition all the while. I swung with all of my might and the glass sort of crackled and sagged away. It was that non-shatter safety glass. Not enough safety for Murdoch. I remember smiling as I smashed his head. Again and again.

I guess that I was still clubbing him when I realized that six squad cars from the Scottsdale Police Department had converged into the, by now, quite crowded cul-de-sac. Lights were flashing and sirens were blaring. I looked around and saw that at least twelve cops had revolvers leveled and pointed. At me.

So, in a nutshell that was it. My incident. It made a big splash in the local papers, and was very hot on the televised news reports. Even CNN carried it for a couple of days. About the same time as the cops showed up, the KTAR traffic copter, having heard the police call, and hovering about two hundred feet overhead, had captured some rather spectacular footage of the carnage and destruction which had befallen this once quiet middle-class suburban street. Four dead bodies, the smoldering hulk of my Lincoln, the prone twenty-two foot saguaro, Murdoch's wrecked Caddy and, of course, the books which Iris had strewn around. All in all, quite a mess.

I was, most naturally, in shock. I vaguely remember having my hands shackled behind my back and being stuffed into the back seat of a patrol car. I remember one of the officers guiding the top of my head as I awkwardly backed into the rear seat of the squad car. He held his hand on my head with palm down so I wouldn't bang my head as I tried to get in. "Careful," he said. "Don't hurt yourself."

"Thank you." I replied.

Part 3
INCARCERATED

The time is really flying now, and although I still need to tell you about my trial and what happened right after the trial, I think you should know at least a little bit about what it was like for me to be imprisoned. In Arizona.

Things were a little hazy right after I was arrested, but I do remember being booked— photographed, fingerprinted and strip-searched at the Maricopa County jail out on Madison Avenue in downtown Phoenix. Just a few blocks from Governor Symington The Third's bankrupt Mercado shopping mall.

I was taken to a cell which I shared with a fellow named Faust Falcone. Faust had been a small-time importer of cheeses, olive oil, sun-dried tomatoes and nine-inch stilettos from his native Sicily. He had owned a small warehouse in one of the more decrepit industrial sections of Apache Junction just southeast of Phoenix, and made a modest living. Trying to expand the territory in which he was doing business, Faust and a couple of his helpers ended up dropping the son of some Mafia kingpin into Lake Powell one night, after tying a couple of fifty pound wheels of Provolone cheese and a little Gorgonzola around this guy's neck. Enraged, the Mafia guy recruited a close friend of Faust and had this false friend lure Faust into an ambush by telling him that they were going to do a simple burglary and maybe a little arson in another local warehouse. Once Faust was inside this warehouse, five Mafia hit men opened fire, hitting him with no less than twenty-one bullets. When the polizei showed up ten minutes later and approached Faust, who now resembled a piece of Swiss cheese, he achieved legendary status among local mobsters by telling the police, "Nobody shot me."

Jailed for attempted burglary and insolence, he was a friendly enough guy to have as a cellmate, but had absolutely no interest in discussing books with me. Aside from flatly stating that Mario Puzo's *Godfather* "was the greatest fuckin' movie ever written," and that Al Pacino "should have gotten the fuckin' Pulitzer Prize," he had no literary background to speak of. Himself awaiting trial, he enjoyed passing his time watching television. His favorite TV program was "The Love Connection" and he went into paroxysms of laughter whenever the host of this show, Chuck Woolery, moued at the camera while the frequently mismatched contestants described the hideous events of a blind date together and tried to outdo each other with stinging barbs and insults. "On national TV," Faust would chortle. "What a bunch of dickheads."

After only sixteen days in the cell with Mr. Falcone, I was suddenly and without warning moved out. In an unprecedented development, Attorney General Grant Woods had arranged for me to be transferred to the state prison here in Florence. Over vehement objections by my attorneys, I was housed here on death row, even before the start of my trial. Citing concern for "the safety of the other prisoners in the penal system," Attorney General Woods had persuaded the Arizona Department of Corrections and a Superior Court judge to mandate this transfer.

Being housed on death row, even before I had been convicted of any crime, left me intimidated as well as confused and depressed. I mean, while the Maricopa County jail hadn't exactly been the Ritz Carlton—no mints placed on your pillow at night, I had sort of settled in. Death row here in Florence seemed much more stark and somber.

The feelings of isolation and abandonment which now overwhelmed me soon had a devastating effect upon my health. I complained to the guards of my nervous tics, insomnia, loss of appetite, excruciating migraines, heart-burn and bedwetting. They told me that these ailments were quite common on "the row," and were, in all proba-bility, stress induced; nothing to worry about. My contin-ued whining about the debilities which afflicted me finally brought results. I was visited in my cell by Warden Butchko's own personal physician, Dr. Hermann Grumbacher. Grumbacher, a man nearing the age of eighty, and a graduate of the medical school at the University of Asunción in his native Paraguay, spoke with a strange teutonic accent and a slight lisp. Sporting both a neatly trimmed goatee and a green-tinted monocle, he made it quite clear that I would not be coddled or other-wise pampered. Following my description of the symp-toms which were troubling me, Grumbacher offered no salves, balms or medication, but stroking his short beard muttered, "Zis iss normal. Zoon zis vill all be ofer vor you."

Remembering Faust's parting advice to me, "Let it roll off your back like a duck," I tried to pull myself out from the depression in which I found myself mired. I began to read some of the many paperbacks which were available to us (hard cover books were forbidden) and soon I began to feel more salubrious. The reading and the frequent but all-too-brief visits from my attorneys made me feel like I was returning to the land of the living and I became determined to rekindle my interest in books and literature. I decided to try to organize a series of literary discussion groups among some of the other inmates on "the row."

These early attempts to involve some of my fellow inmates in an informal series of book discussions met with less than an enthusiastic response. Jesus "Diablo Rojo" Guzman, who had been convicted for his part in an unbelievable crime spree during which he had murdered eleven coffee shop waitresses for what his attorney later characterized as "their terrible service, rudeness, lack of eye make-up and atrocious hair dos," was the first one I approached.

"Mr. Diablo, uh, Mr. Guzman, would you possibly have any interest in joining me and a couple of the other fellows to talk about some of the early works of Proust, or perhaps Thoreau?"

"Fok ju mon. Get da fok otta ma fokkin face."

I immediately realized that Mr. Guzman's use of the word "ju" was not meant as a negative reflection or slur on my Hebraic ancestry, but was merely the Chicano equivalent of the word "you." It was also clear that Mr. Guzman was not really a good candidate for my group and I immediately desisted.

Trying to enhance the appeal of my proposal by broadening the scope of the material to be considered produced no better result. During one of our bi-weekly sessions in the exercise yard, I tried to engage Emmett "Laces" Stokes and Roosevelt Mimms who had been playfully horsing around together. Stokes' nickname "Laces" had come about as a result of his peculiar habit of tying people's shoelaces together after he had, in some gruesome fashion, disposed of them. Mimms, a convicted rapist, kidnapper, arsonist and murderer, was simply known as "Reverend." I suggested to them the possibilities of discussing some of the giants of black American literature such as Baldwin and Ellison, and their relevance to contemporary Afro-American issues and concerns. This overture was rebuffed out of hand by an unrelenting flood of profanities and vulgarisms which, although I cannot remember them verbatim, promised me great bodily harm. I do distinctly recall that Laces pinioned my arms while Reverend Mimms tried to remove my face from its customary position and stick it on my back. I also remember The Reverend telling me that, if I ever got within five hundred feet of him again, he would, "rip off yo' mutha fuggin haid, and spit in yo' mutha fuggin neck."

I scored a minor triumph of sorts, when Lester Sobran agreed to discuss Thomas L. Berger's four volume Carlo Reinhard series with me. Sobran, a native Croatian and former postal worker, was short and fat with Coke bottle thick glasses. Possessed of oily black hair, he spoke only broken English and had never even heard of Berger before my suggestion.

The innumerate Sobran had run amok at the Disneyland theme park in southern California, when, after accusing a clerk at a concession stand of shortchanging him after he had purchased six churros and a lemonade, he had pulled a fully automatic assault weapon called an A-K 47 from a duffel bag and began to mow down customers and park employees alike. Strolling casually from the stunned theme park, he lobbed a hand grenade into the music control room from which they play "It's A Small World After All," and made his escape. Only a few hours later he had been arrested by two alert off-duty Los Angeles plain clothes cops at a Bob's Big Boy on La Cienega Boulevard. Lester had just polished off his customary three quarter-pounders with extra mayo, a double fries, apple pie à la mode and a couple of diet Dr. Peppers and was leaving, when he became abusive toward the cashier who, he felt, had shortchanged him. The officers, who had been quietly snacking on some blueberry blintzes and coffee at a nearby booth, noted the exchange of unpleasantries at the cash register and quickly sprang into action, bludgeoning Sobran into submission, causing slight but irreversible brain damage. Only after Lester was comatose did the officers discover their good fortune, when, upon searching the duffel bag and Sobran's Toyota in the parking lot, they found the spectacular array of weapons contained therein.

Quickly convicted, Lester had been sentenced to eight consecutive death sentences. His defense of temporary insanity had been rejected after the judge, over vociferous objection by defense counsel, had allowed the jury to view a videotape of the events at Disneyland. This videotape, fortuitously shot by a Mr. K. Takashita, a Japanese tourist, showed several of the park's most famous and lovable cartoon characters being blasted by Lester, and diving for cover. This had been too much for the jury, especially the scenes of Pluto expiring in the arms of Sneezy, one of only four surviving dwarfs, and Donald Duck leaping headfirst into a wire trash receptacle.

Immediately following his sentencing in California, Lester had been extradited to Arizona, where he was once again, tried, convicted and sentenced to death for a rampage, equally outrageous, albeit less publicized, committed here in the Grand Canyon State just prior to his star-crossed trip to Disneyland.

Lester had been living with his elderly mother in a very modest home in Weedville, a rural community, about thirty-five miles northwest of Phoenix. One Sunday morning, Lester had arisen at six o'clock looking forward to his customary laid-back Sunday during which he enjoyed reading the colored funnies in the newspaper, drinking a few brewskis and listening to his extraordinarily extensive collection of recordings by Lawrence Welk and Barry Manilow. Going to fetch his Sunday edition of the *Arizona*

Republic, he had been horrified to see his neighbor's small, yappy, brown and white dog, a beagle named Mr. Peebles, urinating on his newspaper. Despite the early hour, Lester, incensed, phoned his neighbor to complain in his own awkward fashion about Mr. Peebles' misconduct.

The neighbor, Mr. Bud Seward, had only recently moved to Weedville, renting the house next door to Lester after leaving his job of fifteen years as an effluent quality control engineer at the Palo Verde Nuclear Generating Station about forty-five miles west of Phoenix. Sending a letter of resignation to his supervisor in which he had stated that he was quitting because his wife had complained "that his pecker was glowing in the dark," Seward had embarked on a new career, selling photographically illustrated versions of the Bible door to door. Anyway, Bud, who had always fancied himself as somewhat of a prankster, sadly underestimated his neighbor Sobran, and, annoyed by the early morning wake up call, decided to retaliate.

Going to his backyard with a brown paper sack, Seward collected some dogshit and after adding a few crumpled sheets of newspaper, stealthily deposited this sack on Lester's front porch. Lighting the top of the paper bag with his Zippo cigarette lighter, Seward rang Lester's doorbell and quickly darted back to the safety of his own dwelling next door. Already quaffing his third Budweiser and wondering who could be calling on him at half past six on a Sunday morning, Sobran flung the door open, only to be greeted by the flaming sack. Possibly the only adult male south of Nova Scotia not to be wise to this old high school prank, Lester became alarmed about the fire and, wearing only terry cloth bedroom slip-ons, began to stomp out the flames; quickly discovering Bud's treachery.

Lester snapped. Doffing his soiled slippers and clad only in his frayed bathrobe, he snatched an Uzi semi-automatic from an umbrella stand near his front door and marched, barefooted, across the graveled driveway which separated his property from the Seward's. Barging through the flimsy rear screen door, he encountered Bud's wife Helen and her mother, Della, who was visiting from Minneapolis. The two women, who had been awakened by Lester's early phone call, were seated at the small, red-marble Formica and chrome dinette in the living room smoking Lucky Strike cigarettes, drinking coffee and lacquering their fingernails. Sobran marched brusquely past them and, raising his seedy robe, squatted and began to take a crap on the carpeting which covered the living room floor. The women began to shriek in unison and Bud, who had smugly returned to the warmth and comfort of his bed, came hurtling down the stairs just as Lester was finishing. Grabbing the Uzi, Lester quickly smoked all three. A hasty but methodical room by room search failed to turn up Mr. Peebles. The wily beagle, at the first indication of hostilities, had squirmed out through the unlatched screen door and after wandering into Lester's house and urinating on the record collection stacked on the floor, had left unobserved, heading north on Broom Street. Sobran reluctantly abandoned the search and left the Seward's by the front door. After strafing Seward's family auto, a teal-green Geo Metro, Lester marched home, and packed a few things including a home made flamethrower into his oversize duffel bag.

The gunfire had awakened Bethel Yates, a slightly eccentric midget and Weedville's only barber, who lived alone in a small bungalow diagonally across the street, and he phoned the Weedville police to report that he had observed Lester shooting the Geo while screaming, "This one's for you, Bud," an obvious perversion of his favorite beer commercial. Weedville Police Chief Al Bulka, infuriated at being awakened at this early hour and incorrectly assuming that this was simply another case of a disgruntled Geo buyer, ignored the call, telling Yates, "Go back to sleep you little piss-ant and mind your own friggin' business."

Sobran, in the meanwhile, had finished gathering a few more items and, after kissing his mother good-bye, had driven away in his brown 1979 Toyota four door sedan. He headed due west on Interstate 10, and only stopped twice—for gas and a couple of bags of snack food at a Texaco station near Goodyear, just west of Phoenix, and at a Der Wienerschnitzel in Blythe, where he hastily consumed a couple of double cheeseburgers, a bratwurst, fried onion rings, and two diet A&W root beers. Upon reaching Route 5, he considered heading north to Los Baños for a meal at Pea Soup Andersen's where he remembered having had an exceptional meatloaf sandwich several years earlier, while on his way to a Western Regional convention of the National Rifle Association being held in San Francisco, which he had attended with his mom. Carefully considering the fact that it was about three hundred miles out of his way, and suddenly remembering that his mashed potatoes had been lumpy, that the peach cobbler à la mode dessert had been slightly soggy, and that he now recalled that Pea Soup Andersen's had possibly shortchanged him, he opted to drive straight through to Disneyland. He arrived there at four o'clock in the afternoon, only about nine hours after his run-in with the Sewards.

Arizona and California spent three and a half years and a combined total of nearly four million dollars of taxpayer's money in Federal Court in a squabble over which state would have the privilege of executing Lester. Finally, the United States Supreme Court, in a bizarre ruling, announced that Arizona should get the first crack at him, because his crime in Arizona predated his contretemps in the Golden State, even if only by a few hours. There had however, been a bitter battle over California's rights. The Justices had generally agreed that "in the interest of justice and for the sake of equity," Lester's remains should be returned to California after his execution in Arizona, for re-execution. Several of the more moderate Justices felt, however, that California's demand for eight re-executions would violate Lester's constitutional protection from cruel and unusual punishment and that only one re-execution should be allowed. Justices Antonin Scalia and William Rehnquist, on the other hand, obviously deeply and personally touched by the deaths of Dopey, Grumpy and Sleepy, felt that California's demand for eight re-executions was warranted under the circumstances. In a dazzling display of previously well-concealed Solomon-like judicial brilliance, Justice Clarence Thomas forged a compromise, under the terms of which California would be allowed only a single re-execution, but then would be allowed to imprison Sobran's remains for up to seven hundred years. Lester savored that as "a great victory."

I led off our first and regrettably our last discussion about Thomas Berger's eponymous hero, Carlo Reinhard, by inquiring of Lester whether he had any opinion as to the possibility that *Vital Parts* may have been in any way autobiographical. Sobran contributed little, but seemed to mark his agreement with, or disapproval of, my commentary with a series of grunts and belches, and by occasionally breaking wind. After about one half hour, he grunted twice and let loose with an astonishing salvo of flatulence. That seemed to signify the end of his participation for that day; he simply flashed me his crocodilian grin and waddled away.

Sadly, Lester Sobran was executed (for the first time) after only one meeting of our fledgling society.

Apparently Warden Butchko, Governor Symington The Third and the Arizona Board of Pardons and Paroles had all chosen to ignore the many letters I had sent to them on Lester's behalf.

My sorrow over Lester's passing was slightly tempered when I was informed by one of the guards of the circumstances of the execution. For his last meal, Lester had eschewed his favorite foods, hamburgers or anything deep fried, in favor of an extra-large pizza topped with onion, anchovies and green peppers and accompanied by a side order of refried beans with jalapeño peppers obtained by the prison from Los Dos Cucharachas Mexican restaurant about four miles north of Florence. The ingestion of these foods had been craftily calculated by Lester to exacerbate the borborygmus and gastritis which for years had enabled him to excel in the art of passing gas and, as Lester was being strapped to the gurney, he unleashed a barrage of flatulence so intense that the guards were driven from his cell. It had taken Warden Butchko nearly twenty minutes to rally his disheveled troops and, although the execution had finally been completed, it occured almost twenty-five minutes behind schedule. Attorney General Woods, standing and waiting with the witnesses as usual, had been furious. Good old Lester. He had not gone down without a fight. Guns blazing to the end.

With my trial set to begin in about three weeks, I felt it imperative that I keep my spirits up. I dispatched a note to Lenny over at College Used Books and asked him to send me some paperbacks in a light vein. I asked for anything he might have by James Thurber, P.G. Wodehouse, Thorne Smith, A.J. Liebling, S.J. Perlman, Ludwig Bemelmans or Montague Glass. Within days, a small box containing a dozen such paperbacks arrived at my cell. The box had been opened for security inspection, and I noticed the

neatly typed invoice lying atop the books. Good old Lenny.
A true friend; he had billed me on open account despite
my failure to pay his last seventeen such invoices. I was
pleased to see that he had still allowed me the standard
twenty percent discount given to dealers but chagrined to
note that, unlike the earlier invoices, this one reflected a
charge of seven percent for sales tax. Maricopa county had
revoked my bookdealer's resale permit.

Part 4
THE TRIAL

Y ou know that old saw, "The condemned man ate a hearty meal?" Well, don't believe it. I haven't eaten a hearty meal since I was sentenced and especially not this afternoon. Also, I'd like to clear up a little general misunderstanding about the final meal. Everybody thinks that when you're about to be executed you get your choice of anything that you want. Not true. At least a month ago I told the guards that I wanted some stuffed kishka with mushroom gravy, a nice piece of smoked whitefish, some potato latkes and a little noodle kugel for dessert. They laughed good naturedly and flipped me the bird.

At seven o'clock this morning, I was told that I could have anything I wanted but from a choice of four items. Tacos and burritos, pizza, chicken-fried steak or fried chicken. I have figured out that they acquire this cuisine from the Taco Bell, Denny's, Kentucky Fried Chicken and Godfather's Pizza Parlor which line the east side of the highway about two miles north of the prison's main gate. The guards all kept recommending the pizza especially with the extra thick crust. I had heard rumors that Warden Butchko's son-in-law owned a half interest in the pizza parlor and went for the chicken-fried steak instead. Very high in cholesterol but, at this point, what the hell.

The prison doctor left my cell a few minutes ago. He ignored me when I asked him if they would rub my arm with an alcohol swab for hygienic purposes before giving me the needle and seemed a bit apologetic for even bothering me. He checked my heart, blood pressure (which was, not surprisingly, a bit on the high side) and mainly looked over the veins on my arm. They like to make sure that you have a good vein into which they can stick their fucking needle. Can you imagine? These people are going to murder me in less then an hour and they are worried about my blood pressure. I was lucky they didn't send a proctologist.

All of which means that I've got to get this wrapped up in a hurry.

I'll skip all of the pretrial business. Which is boring to begin with. My ex-wife came to see me on my third day in custody and I told her to get into the house and remove all of the books. This left me with zero assets, and a couple of nice kids from the Public Defender's office were assigned to handle my defense.

I was charged with one count of attempted robbery and four counts of murder in the first degree. Right, four counts. In other words, Attorney General Woods was holding me responsible for everything. Even for Louisa Fanner who got crunched by Murdoch's car. The old felony murder routine. In other words, because they said I was trying to commit a robbery of the books, I had committed a felony and the law is that if anyone dies during the commission of a felony the perpetrator of the felony is responsible. In spades.

I don't have time to dwell on this too much, but it's pretty amazing stuff. I tried to help my attorneys out by doing a little legal research for them using the prison's law library and found a couple of Arizona cases which pretty well show you the kind of trouble I was in. In one case two shmoes go to stick up a liquor store. Schmo number one goes in and the other waits outside in the car with the motor running. Schmo number one tells the shopkeeper to stick 'em up. Instead, the guy pulls out a gun and shoots schmo number one in his tracks. Schmo number two, sitting out in the car, gets arrested and convicted of first degree murder. Felony murder rule.

Case number two was even better. A couple of schvartzes walk into a furniture store in Tucson. The first guy says, "Everybody relax and nobody will get hurt." The owner, a guy about eighty years old and with a quadruple bypass, has the big one on the spot. Again, felony murder and both schvartzes get the gas.

As I told you earlier, Needles himself prosecuted for the state. A rotten human being but he really knew the prosecuting business. He waltzed and pirouetted around that courtroom like he owned it. He really seemed to be enjoying the show. First, he called the lab guys, the investigating officers, the coroner, etc. They all testified as to what happened, and how all these people ended up dead. Lots of grisly forensic medical stuff. Replete with gory photos of the victims and what Needles kept calling "the scene of the carnage." All in all, pretty gruesome and unpleasant stuff.

Needles' next witnesses were about a dozen upstanding citizens from northern Illinois who told the court everything you could ever want to know about the Murdoch family. And more. Murdoch and his sister were descended from a U.S. senator from Illinois. Their father had owned a couple of paper mills up in southern Wisconsin, and later had gone into the banking business. Evan Murdoch had run the banks for many years before he retired a couple of years ago. Sister Evelyn, never married, had been involved mostly with charitable work. Iris, who grew up in Milwaukee, had majored in journalism at the University of Chicago. A strident animal rights activist, she had spent several years as a freelance writer before meeting and marrying Evan Murdoch in 1961. They all spent their winters together in Scottsdale. Usually from right after Thanksgiving until the end of April. They were regular churchgoers. Very well heeled. Blah. Blah. Pretty mundane stuff and as Jerry Shaver, my lead attorney, said, "Nothing we didn't expect."

But the next day came a few things that we **didn't** expect. Testimony from three family members including Murdoch's thirty-one year old daughter that neither the Murdochs nor Evelyn had ever had any interest in antiques of any kind. Also, they testified that Murdoch kept only a very small library which consisted almost exclusively of books about the history of Champlain County in Illinois and about the history of the paper making industry. Iris' reading was limited almost exclusively to periodicals concerned with her various animal rights crusades. Not a stick of fiction in the house. Same went for sister Evelyn. She read very little and when she did it was mostly religious material. She also seemed to enjoy an occasional book about British history. But then came a couple of bombshells.

The next couple of witnesses were almost too good to be true. One antique dealer and two members of Murdoch's country club all of whom testified that on several occasions Mr. and Mrs. Murdoch had purchased large quantities of books from them. But only fiction. That was it. Fiction. In average condition. Nothing special. The purchases had been made periodically over the past ten years and involved literally thousands and thousands of books. I noticed that Jerry and my number two attorney, Karen Fishbein, kept looking at each other. What the hell was going on here? Jerry's objection to this testimony as "irrelevant" was met with a withering look from Judge Vaughn. I was confused. I mean, why had he objected? All of this talk that the Murdochs bought lots of books backed up my side of the story. That they were book mavens and hustlers too. They knew exactly what they had been doing to old Mrs. Deutch. Rip-off artists.

There had been a break for lunch following this puzzling testimony, and Jerry and Karen joined me in the holding cell just off the main corridor behind the courtroom. Karen sat on the only chair, legs crossed demurely, as she dejectedly picked at a wilted green salad with a white plastic fork. Jerry joined me on the floor and wolfed down a thick corned beef on rye. As a special treat for me, he had obtained permission to bring my lunch in, although he had been forced to have the food unwrapped and examined before I could receive it. I noticed a very large thumbprint in my chopped liver but ate it anyway. We talked as we ate. Neither of them had liked the smell of this testimony. Jerry was concerned because Murdoch had generally bought the books sight unseen. He had never asked to inspect the books and never haggled over the price. He had always arranged for the books to be delivered to a small private warehouse he owned on Dupont Street in South Chicago where he kept a couple of nice old Packard cars which had belonged to his father. Payment had always been prompt. A check in the mail.

After lunch we returned to court and waited for Needles to call his next witness. "The State calls Major Harley Crenshaw, U.S. Army, Retired."

Jerry was on his feet in a heartbeat. "Objection your honor! Objection! The defense objects to this witness!"

Meanwhile, Major Crenshaw, U.S. Army Retired, was walking briskly toward the witness stand. He waited patiently while Jerry objected until his lips turned blue. The objection was based primarily on the fact that the prosecution had failed to give us notice that they were going to call this witness. Such notice was normally required in order to prevent unfair surprises for which the defense had not been able to prepare. "Objection based on failure to notify, objection based on surprise, based on deceit, based on treachery . . . ."

Needles interrupted quietly and to quote Mark Twain, "with the calm confidence of a Christian holding four aces."

"Your honor, the prosecution only learned of this man's relationship with the deceased early this morning."

One thing about Needles. He could really bullshit with the best of them. I mean, this guy Crenshaw was from Alexandria, Virginia. Had they flown him in on the Concorde? Had he come by fax? No problem for Needles. The major had been right here in Arizona all along. Needles had, quite fortuitously, found him staying at the Princess Hotel right in Scottsdale. Attending a golfing tournament.

"Objection overruled," said the judge. "Swear the witness."

Major Harley Crenshaw, U.S. Army Retired, had been standing, ramrod straight, waiting for a resolution of the conflict. Dressed in his parade uniform, with a chest full of medals and ribbons, he looked a great deal like a shorter version of Michael Redgrave. With a neat hairline mustache. Jerry wondered out loud whether Crenshaw always packed his wool ceremonial full-dress uniform for golf tournaments. In Arizona. In August. Judge Vaughn glared at him.

Major Crenshaw testified crisply and authoritatively. He seemed to anticipate every question and had a clear, concise answer. It almost seemed rehearsed. But he sure came off well. I, about to be buried by this military putz, found myself admiring his cool direct approach. "Yes," he had served in active duty, "Yes," he had graduated from West Point, "Yes," he still maintained a close relationship with the Pentagon. Pentagon? In what capacity? As a special liaison to the Department of Veteran's Affairs. "No," he was not paid for his work with the department, just his normal military pension benefits. "Yes," he had known Evan Murdoch. How long? For over forty years. Jerry objected again.

Judge Vaughn, seemingly enchanted with the major, made his ruling: "Shut up Shaver. Shut up and stay shut up."

Crenshaw had gone to a military prep academy with Murdoch. It was a small private school on the shores of Lake Superior and was very, very exclusive. Crenshaw had been appointed to West Point and Murdoch, having decided to follow his father into the banking business, had matriculated at the University of Chicago. School of Management and Finance. Fate had reunited them in 1952, when Murdoch had been drafted into the service and had been sent to serve in Korea. A corporal, he had been assigned to the 39th Infantry in which Crenshaw had been a young lieutenant. Needles was about to spring the trap. It went exactly like this:

> *Needles:* Major Crenshaw, several witnesses have testified here that Mr. and Mrs. Murdoch have, for at least the past eight years, purchased large accumulations of books or libraries of literature and fiction, which Mr. Murdoch always had delivered to his warehouse on Dupont Street in Chicago
>
> *Crenshaw:* That is correct, sir. Yes, yes he bought books.
>
> *Needles:* Major, do you know anything about these

books? What happened to them?

Crenshaw: Those books were for me, sir. Evan Murdoch bought those books to give to me.

Needles: (incredulously) For you Major? I don't understand. Would you please explain.

Crenshaw: Yes, yes of course. Part of my work with the Veteran's Administration is involved with what we refer to as Facility Services. FACSERV. We try to provide extra services to our facilities which would otherwise not be provided because of certain budgetary constraints.

Needles: And by facilities, Major, are you referring to the hospitals run by the Veteran's Administration?

Crenshaw: I am, sir.

Needles: And when you refer to extra services, Major, do you include such services as providing books for the patients to read?

Crenshaw: I do, sir.

Needles: Are you testifying here this afternoon, Major, that Evan Murdoch bought these books with his own funds, and donated them to VA hospitals for the use and enjoyment of the patients in those institutions.

Crenshaw: I am, sir.

The rest of Crenshaw's testimony concerned Murdoch's tour in Korea. Crenshaw had been leading a platoon on a night patrol about fifty kilometers east of Inchon through a torrential downpour when they had been spotted and pinned down by a Red Chinese machine gun nest. Murdoch had, on his own initiative and despite withering machine gun and rocket fire, belly-crawled through muck and mire to single-handedly flank and take out the enemy position. Hit by shrapnel from a potato-masher grenade,

Murdoch had been horribly wounded but was miraculously kept alive and rehabilitated at a VA facility in Seoul where he had been rushed by Jeep. His left leg had been amputated at the knee. Which of course accounted for his dreadful limp.

That did it. Jerry slumped in his seat and Karen stared at her fingernails. Not only was this Murdoch not a goniff, he was a **fucking war hero**. Decorated by General Douglas MacArthur himself. The books over which he died were not for profit but were to be donated as reading material for the poor bastards who wind up in the VA hospitals . Oh shit!

It only got a little worse. Crenshaw went on to describe how every year good old Evan would call him and tell him to get a truck over to the warehouse on Dupont Street and how Murdoch would, despite his physical limitations, actually help load the boxed books onto the trucks side by side with VA personnel. The only demand Murdoch made was that this arrangement be kept strictly between them (Mr. and Mrs. Murdoch) and Major Crenshaw. No publicity or thanks. Crenshaw dabbed at his eyes as his testimony concluded. The jury stared at me with loathing and disgust. Juror number nine, a burly, retired copper miner wearing a red and black checkered flannel shirt with wide navy blue suspenders, had to be physically restrained by the bailiff as he tried to lunge at me from the jury box. Jerry's calls for a mistrial were unavailing as Judge Vaughn tried to restore order to the courtroom by banging his gavel—again and again and again—until it shattered.

Old Mrs. Deutch's testimony wasn't exactly helpful either. You remember her. Granny. Spry and sprightly as ever. She told the court about her late husband Augustus "Gus" Deutch. They had met and married in Milwaukee back in the '30s. Gus Deutch had worked in the public library system through the depression years, eventually heading up the acquisition department. He had had a life-long obsession with books and literature and had, against her wishes, spent a fair part of their income on books. He had established close and special relationships with a number of publishers in his varied capacities with the library over the years and had often been sent "new books" as gifts. Strictly speaking, these books were the property of the Milwaukee Public Library system and accepting these gratuities was against the rules, but with nobody being the wiser, Gus had kept them anyway. He had been fanatical in preserving these books and had gone to extreme lengths to keep them clean, dry and away from the delete-rious effects of the ultraviolet rays of the sun. She had had no idea of the value of Gus' collection. She did not know how many books he had in the boxes. But she did know that Louisa and Eddie, her husband, had helped her pack up only that part of the collection that Gus had called "trade editions." She had left "the junk," or what the late Gus Deutch had always called "galleys or proofs" and "advance copies" from his publishing pals (mostly, as she said, "kind of like old-time paperbacks") packed away in her garage in Sun City. She wasn't sure, but she thought she had about thirty cartons of these proofs. I started to become dizzy and faint but still noticed a con-siderable stirring in the courtroom upon that revelation. A number of the local booksellers who had been attend-ing the trial on a daily basis had, moving at warp speed, vanished from the courtroom.

Granny's testimony had been simple and straightfor-ward. She had missed most of the action. (Needles had referred to it as "the massacre," and Judge Vaughn had sus-tained Jerry's objection.) She had gone back into Louisa's house to "call the Sheriff as soon as I saw that man," pointing her bony finger in my direction, "tryin' to steal the poor lady's books. " She had been talking, of course, about my failed attempt to rescue *Crazy In Berlin* from Iris.

Needles paused here and tilted his head back. He closed his eyes, pursed his lips and then broke into a sardonic grin as he rocked back and forth on his cordovan wing tips. His hands were clasped behind his back as he took a deep breath and said, "That's all your honor. The State rests."

At the noon recess for lunch I wasn't interested in the tongue on rye (with brown mustard) which Jerry had brought for me. He finished his brisket sandwich with potato salad on the side and began to work on mine. Karen, by now near tears, had barely touched her fruit salad with yogurt. We talked about trying to reach a plea bargain with Needles. Jerry felt that it would be a gigantic waste of time.

While about eighty-five percent of all criminal cases in Arizona are settled by a plea bargain, Needles had, from the start, refused to make any offer on this one. All of Jerry's early approaches had been met with one rebuff after another. True, Needles had dropped the additional charge of driving with expired tags on my license plates, but we did not view this as much of a concession since I had a canceled check from the Motor Vehicle Department confirming my timely payment. The tags had, as usual, been misaddressed. It turned out of course, that Needles both **wanted** and **needed** to prosecute this matter. He intended to enter the race for Governor of Arizona and there was no better way for him to get daily news coverage. The three week trial was just what the doctor had ordered. Nearly a month of free TV coverage. He took full advantage. Always impeccably attired, Needles sported a spectacular succession of Hugo Boss, double-breasted, lightweight wool worsted and gabardine suits. Navy blues and charcoal greys with neat pinstriping and finished with crisp-white and pale-blue dress shirts, his entwined initials boldly emblazoned on the luxurious French cuffs. And leather thong bola ties, fastened at the throat with the traditional southwestern-style clasp fashioned from turquoise and silver. I noted, with a touch of queasiness, that for his final summation to the jury, he had changed to a clasp made of clear Lucite with the remains of a rather large scorpion embedded therein.

For nearly three hours he vilified me, ranting and raving about, and I quote: "brutal savagery, loathsome predators, mad-dog killers in our midst, depraved degenerates," and so on. He also made much political hay with the issue of the safety and welfare of the elderly snowbirds who flocked to the valley each winter. Like the Murdochs. These snowbirds were mostly rude but wealthy old farts from the Midwest—who, although disruptive to the daily lives of ordinary citizens—with their atrocious driving and abominable lack of manners, represented a wellspring of riches for local merchants. The valley's very economic survival depended upon their annual migration. So, you can see that Jerry had a point. Needles would literally have laughed at any suggestion of a plea bargain. After, I mean, we had heard from Granny and Major Crenshaw. I was cooked.

We tried. Three witnesses appeared for the defense. My former wife—who, on the Monday following the incident had submitted an application to restore her maiden name, told the jury how I had been primarily a vegetarian for humane reasons and how I had refused to allow her to kill even the most annoying bug or pest in our home. She explained that I had developed an elaborate method for the live capture of every disgusting insect which invaded our home, trapping these hideous creatures in a Tupperware container fitted with a lucite top which allowed me to release my quarry unharmed to the great outdoors, where it belonged. Her testimony was supposed to help convince the jury that I was, by nature, a harmless and gentle man. The jury however, seemed less than impressed. Following her testimony, I noticed several members of the panel, especially the five women, peering at me warily out of the corners of their eyes.

I've already told you about poor Lenny Warman. He, unlike the remainder of my "former colleagues," had been able to visualize the insane desperation which had brought on my ill-fated attempt to get the books away from Mrs. Murdoch or anyone else who might abuse or maltreat them. As I mentioned before, his testimony was met with such virulent hostility that he slunk from the courtroom, a shattered man. He left nearly in tears and stared straight ahead on his way out. He refused to even cast a glance in my direction and thus failed to see me flash him the old thumbs-up sign.

Grasping at straws and against his better judgment, Jerry agreed with my suggestion to call as a witness my last remaining friend in Arizona, Wolf Griller. Griller had amassed a fortune as a leading breeder and trainer of greyhound racing dogs, but had been forced out of the business after he had been indicted on charges of fraud, deceit and the improper use of kosher cold cuts. Several former employees had turned him in for having fed large quantities of a mixture of smoked salmon laced with Hebrew National salami to his hounds the day before they were to race. The resulting thirst would cause them to imbibe quantum amounts of water on race day which slowed them down so much that they sometimes appeared to be running in slow motion. Other evidence confirmed that Griller had, on many occasions, applied liberal amounts of

Simonize automotive wax to the pads of his dog's feet just prior to a race. It was established that he had engaged in these nefarious schemes while wagering on the other pooches, allowing his own to suffer ignominious defeat.

Barred from the racing business for life, Griller had lost the balance of his fortune when, trying to capitalize on his own notoriety, he opened a chain of nineteen do-it-yourself picture framing shops called I WAS FRAMED. This venture went Tapioca City only eleven weeks after the date of the Grand Opening.

I had met and befriended Griller at one of my former haunts, the Hadassah Woman's Auxiliary Thrift Store on South Central. I had been engaged in my usual search for rare first editions and Griller, thoroughly discredited and impecunious, was lurking around and scouring the bins for salvageable underwear and socks. I took pity on him and invited him to join me for a coffee next door at Nick's Argosy Cafe, a greasy, Greek owned, hole-in-the-wall, which featured the world's most rotten souvlaki. I was shocked as I watched him devour the crackers from the little wicker basket and then mix ketchup from the bottle on the table into the cup of hot water supplied by our snaggle-toothed but obliging waitress. Adding salt and pepper, he slurped it noisily. Ignoring his paper napkin, Griller smiled and belched as he wiped his lips on his frayed sleeve and grunted, "I like tomato soup."

I introduced him to the writings of Thomas Berger, and we actually formed a two-member T. L. Berger fan club. (We had considered approaching Lenny Warman as a prospective member, but decided in the negative. The uxorious Warman had a family, and wasn't free to join us for our weekly meetings which we generally held about eleven o'clock P.M. at Tiffany's Club For Gentlemen out on the corner of Scottsdale Road and Shea Boulevard.) Griller had, not unlike myself, become obsessed with Berger's work and polished off all eighteen novels in one marathon sitting. It took him thirty-four weeks. He finally declared *Neighbors*, which had been made into a movie starring John Belushi and Dan Ackroyd, to be the greatest book ever written and he reread it at regular intervals. At last count, he was on his tenth time around.

Needles tore poor Wolf to shreds on cross-examination. Untidy and slovenly by nature, Griller's poor personal hygiene habits became glaring deficiencies as he squirmed on the witness stand. Needles produced a "rap sheet" about which I had known nothing, and proceeded to establish for the jury that Griller had a long history of arrests for public indecency and related morals charges. Particularly damaging, as well as embarrassing, was Griller's admission that he had twice been arrested for having exposed himself in front of the orangutan cage at the Phoenix Zoological Gardens. These additional charges of lewd and lascivious conduct had been dropped in return for Griller's guilty pleas to the lesser charges of cruelty to animals. Furthermore, Griller had, on no less than seven prior occasions, been arrested for violent attacks on members of the Arizona State Sun Devil Pep Band as they performed at home basketball games. Griller, it seemed, lost all control at the sight of female trombone players.

Following Needles' devastating cross examination, Wolf left the stand red-faced but triumphant. Jerry told me that Wolf had flashed me a furtive double thumbs-up sign as he passed by us at the defense table. I hadn't seen it since I had my face buried in my palms.

So there you have it. It couldn't have gone worse. For me. The jury's verdict was not unexpected. Only the speed with which it was reached was a surprise. Six minutes. At a "post-trial celebration," held at the elegant Arizona

Biltmore and sponsored jointly by the Murdoch's three children and the Scottsdale Chamber of Commerce, one of the jurors being interviewed by a reporter for the *Scottsdale Progress* was quoted as saying, "If one of the lady jurors hadn't insisted on redoing her make up they could have been back in three."

Scottsdale's mayor for the past twenty-six years, Mr. Herb Drinkwater, who himself was considering a run for governor against Mr. Symington The Third, citing his vast business expertise as the former operator of a now defunct wine and cheese shop, was one of the featured speakers at this gala. Mayor Drinkwater, sort of the Will Rogers of western mayors, had never met a developer he didn't like. Under Herb's stewardship the once quaint and beautiful town of Scottsdale, with trails for horseback riding and glorious desert vistas and preserves, had been transformed into a smog-laden, traffic-snarled, mini-version of Los Angeles.

By nature a taciturn man, rarely speaking extemporaneously for more then four or five hours at a time, Herb always countered the environmentalists or "eco-terrorists," as he referred to them, with a few well-chosen words. When called upon to defend the policies which had resulted in the devastation of millions of acres of irreplaceable natural habitat and the annihilation of innumerable species of native flora and fauna, Herb invariably pointed with pride to the sardine-like rows of cheap tract housing which stretched to the horizon and said, "Hey buckaroo, mountain lions and coyotes don't buy houses."

Anyway, chugging his sixth flute of Dom Perignon champagne, Drinkwater, who billed himself "mayor of the West's most western town," proposed a toast to "the entire Scottsdale Police Department for their brilliant detective work in solving this case." When a reporter from the

Tucson Star Democrat pointed out that the incident had been viewed by fifty-six eyewitnesses and that I had surrendered peacefully on the spot, Drinkwater began nervously fingering his trademark twin pearl-handled colt revolvers and told him to "stick his notebook where the sun don't shine," and to "git out of town before sundown."

Obviously upset by this minor set-to with a respected member of the paparazzi, Drinkwater switched off of the champagne and ordered up a couple of quick "shooters." These rather potent libations are the Arizona version of the ever popular east coast "boilermaker," except that instead of straight whiskey followed by a beer chaser, the potion out here consists of tequila with beer. Absolutely correct Arizona protocol requires that these be imbibed in a strict ritualistic sequence of squeezing lime juice onto the back of the hand, pouring salt onto the lime juice, licking the salt and juice off of the back of the hand, drinking the shot of tequila in one gulp, biting into the remains of the lime while conjuring up the most horrible grimace possible and then chugging the glass of beer. Anyway, Herb, working on his fourth shooter, had mixed up the sequence and was trying to drink directly out of the saltshaker when Marshall Randall, his pimple-faced nineteen year old nephew and $45,000 per year "aide," reminded him that sundown had actually occurred several hours earlier and that the reporter was still hanging around snacking on swedish meatballs, cold lasagna and Jello-mold at the hors d'oeuvre table. Drinkwater was clearly flustered and more or less shit-faced. He swivelled slowly on his salmon-colored, emu-skin cowboy boots, scowled savagely at Randall and snarled, "Pipe down and mind your own beeswax you little jerk-off."

As you know by now, all of our appeals fell on deaf ears. Particularly stinging was the rejection, by the United States

Supreme Court, of our petition for habeas corpus. By a nine to nothing margin. Chief Justice Rehnquist and Associate Justice Sandra Day O'Conner, both natives of my adopted state of Arizona, felt it necessary to assail our petition as a "frivolous importunity by a demented and repugnant defendant." Justice Clarence Thomas went a step further and, in what some legal scholars later criticized as excessively harsh language, referred to me as "an unrepentant motherfucker."

In hindsight, we had some second thoughts about our decision to eschew an insanity defense. It's not that we hadn't seriously considered that as a viable option. I had certainly been at least somewhat deranged when the incident went ballistic. The dilemma that we had faced was simple. On April 9th, only one week before that fateful day, Governor Symington The Third had pushed a bill through the Arizona legislature called *The Morrow Act.* Under that new law the State of Arizona would no longer accept a plea of NOT GUILTY BY REASON OF INSANITY. Anyone wanting to justify or excuse his or her actions by claiming that they were not in their right minds at the time, would now have to plead GUILTY, BUT INSANE. The sentencing guidelines were also revised so that anyone entering such a plea would automatically be sentenced to serve the same amount of time as he would have normally received; however, instead of going to prison, the sentence would be served in a maximum security institution for the criminally insane. No real bargain as far as I was concerned. I would have had to serve almost 500 years in such a place. Considering what regular walking around Arizonans are like, I had no interest in hanging around with those on the inside. And especially not for 500 years.

Part 5
THE AFTERMATH

I've pretty well brought you up to date. Which is just as well, since I only have a few minutes left. The actual execution isn't for another thirty-three minutes but the festivities begin about twenty minutes before. That's when they check my pulse and blood pressure for the twenty-third time today and strap me onto the gurney on which they cart me into the execution room. They don't call it a chamber any more. A room. Sounds more gentile. Like I give a shit what they call it. Some of the other guys here on the row call it "Going to the Woods' shed." More dark humor.

Also, this is the time when they put a syringe into my arm and start a flow of saline solution going into me. Sort of warming up. Then, at exactly five minutes past midnight, they substitute the hard stuff for the saline. With just a flick of the wrist. Say what you will, these Arizonans have got it down. They used to do hanging, but in the 1930s went to cyanide and now here in the '90s, lethal injection. Arizona. Perpetually forty-eighth out of fifty states in per capita spending on education, but in the vanguard when it comes to execution technology.

Rabbi Blinder, my chaplain, had come this morning to ask if I felt like davening. I told him that I would, but only with the traditional tallis and tephillin. He actually asked Warden Butchko for permission to bring me these sacraments, but the warden felt that there was too much risk. I might be able to hang myself with the tallis, or the rabbi might try to smuggle me a few Valiums or quaaludes in the little boxes on the tephillin. Where the parchment with the Holy Prayers are stuffed. Butchko, in an unprecedented display of generosity, did tell Blinder that a yarmulke would be okay.

I told the rabbi to bag the yarmulke, because I didn't want too much made of the fact that I was a Jew. It could do nothing but bring disgrace to other Arizona Jews. Already an oppressed minority, you had to walk almost thirty feet before finding a bagel shop or kosher style deli in Scottsdale. Blinder told me that "when it was time," I should inhale deeply. This, he said, would make it go faster and easier. They had forgotten to tell him that they had switched from gas. Also, rabbis don't seem to have much practice with this type of matter. Very few Jewish mass murderers. It's pretty much a goyish activity.

Anyway, when my guard from the day shift left at three o'clock this afternoon, he seemed saddened by the whole sordid affair. One of the few Oriental correctional officers in the system, his name was Lawrence Wong. We had actually developed a rather good relationship over the past couple of months, and I thought I saw a tear coursing down his cheek. I usually gave him a chipper "So long Wong," as he left each day but this time I simply said, "Good-bye Larry." He in turn clasped my hand and responded with "Take it easy man." Much more appropriate than his customary "Have a good one."

Oh shit! I hear them coming with the gurney. It has a squeaky wheel. "Big Red" Dolan in the next cell just yelled, "Hey, didn't you assholes ever hear about WD 40?" What a way to go. On a gurney with a squeaky wheel. I've only got a minute or two left now and there were a few last things I wanted to let you in on.

Most important was the books. The goddamned books. My undoing. Every day during the trial I saw the books. No, not in my mind. For real. They had all been introduced as evidence. By that schmuck Needles. The unopened cartons had been stacked up on a huge library gurney, also with a squeaky wheel, and were schlepped into and out of the courtroom every day of the trial. Each box had a big yellow sticker on it which said PROPERTY OF THE MARICOPA COUNTY SHERIFF. EVIDENCE LOCKER. And a hand written number on each sticker which said "People's Exhibit #1, #2, #3, etc." I remember that on April 16th there had been twenty-one boxes. I don't know what had happened in the meanwhile, but now there were only fifteen boxes left. Still unopened. The loose books which had spilled out on the street were also labeled as People's Exhibits. Some total retardo in the Sheriff's Department had actually stamped each book with a rubber stamp. On the inside. Ruined. *Crazy in Berlin* looked like it had been in a train wreck. And I had to look at it every day during the trial.

The books had been kept as evidence for almost two years after my trial was over. Until all of my substantive appeals were over. Meanwhile, there had been tons of civil litigation over who should get them. The Murdoch estate sued old lady Deutch. The old lady sued the Murdochs. The Milwaukee Public Library sued everybody. The old lady had never cashed the check. I guess that she was too upset when the banks opened two days later. The Murdoch's estate claimed that she had accepted payment and that title to the books had passed to Evan and Iris when she took hold of the check. The case is still going on, and I'll never know who won. Too bad. I have a lot invested in those books. I'll never get to go through the remaining boxes. I'd sure have liked to find out if there was a copy of *The Postman Always Rings Twice.*

As for the cartons of uncorrected proofs and advance reading copies in old Mrs. Deutch's garage out in Sun City, which had to be worth at least five million dollars, they had mysteriously vanished by the end of the day during which she testified about their existence. One of her neighbors, Mrs. Martha Dockweiler, a widow in her early nineties with thinning, bluish, permed hair and failing eyesight reported that she wasn't sure, but that she thought she saw a light metallic blue Dodge van cruising around that afternoon.

EPILOGUE
By Rabbi Jacob Blinder

The execution was carried out as scheduled. I learned this sad news from the one o'clock A.M. newscast on KPHO TV, Channel 5. The live report, telecast from just outside the prison grounds at Florence, was short and simple. In the background I could clearly see Attorney General Woods passing out cigars to a number of reporters gathered around him.

The morning after these lugubrious events, the unfortunate man's nearly destitute former wife called at my office and sought my assistance in sending his remains back to Cheektowaga, New York, his birthplace, for a proper burial in a Jewish cemetery. Without hesitation I wrote her a check for $2,500 from our synagogue's emergency family-relief fund.

This fund, which is supported by private donations and by several annual fund-raisers sponsored by our Temple's Sisterhood, was replenished a few months later by the proceeds of a wonderfully successful book sale. Ruth Eppler, president of the Sisterhood, and her husband Mort had most generously donated their entire library of almost six hundred books to this sale. The Epplers had acquired this marvelous collection during their forty year marriage. From the Book Of The Month Club.